CLEAN AND COLD
APPLIANCE REPAIR

❄

D1738721

CLEAN AND COLD
APPLIANCE REPAIR

❄

Mimi Ahern

First Edition, June 2013

Copyright © 2012 Mimi Ahern

This is a work of fiction. Names, characters, places and incidents either are the product of the author's imagination or are used fictitiously.

ISBN-13:978-1484893753
ISBN-10: 1484893751

This book is dedicated to
Janet Geraty

Acknowledgements

I am deeply grateful to Lou and Lorie Boris. They gave of their time and experiences, generously and lovingly. I hope my small effort honors a great man, and his devoted wife.

Many thanks to my editors Cathy Thompson, Esther Hilferty, Janet Geraty, and Jeff Shafe. You all made a difference to this starfish.

In gratitude to Malone, Jackie and Gary for giving me their quiet support, even doing laundry without being asked.

Finally, I am grateful to my husband, Mike. Hc has been the best part in the book of my life.

CLEAN AND COLD
APPLIANCE REPAIR
❄

One

FRUITS OF THE SEASON

ON ONE SIDE of town, Mae was hot under the collar. The weather was only partly to blame. She knelt in front of the planter bed which her husband Frank had framed with old railroad ties. The planters were in the front yard not the backyard because of the neighbor's dog. During peak gardening hours, the dog perched on his porch with one eye open and both ears pricked. If he caught sight or sound of a stranger, he released a cacophony of barks and threatening displays of aggression.

Safely in the front yard, Mae scoured her tomato plants, but found no ripe tomatoes. Just a few days ago, there were so many red tomatoes she had planned a meal around them in anticipation. She furrowed her brow and looked suspiciously around the neighborhood.

She removed the straw hat she wore to keep the sun from her fair skin, and returned the silver curl on her forehead to its proper position behind her ear. She would need help to fix the disappearing tomato problem and she knew just the man for the job.

She stood stiffly, using the planter bed for support. The twinge between her shoulder blades did not discourage her. Instead, she kindly reminded herself a younger person would have trouble with the awkward positions gardening required.

Empty basket in hand, her long legs quickly covered the distance from the planter, over the lawn, to the path that led to the front porch. She kicked off her clogs and went into the cool shade of her home. She hung her hat by its string on the coat hook and found Frank where she left him.

"You are not going to believe this!" Mae announced, with a dramatic flair she reserved for non-emergencies. Her husband, Frank, sat at the small, round kitchen table wearing the clean, green work shirt Mae had pressed for him. Forms and papers were stacked neatly in several piles around his glowing laptop. He tapped the keyboard and added numbers to an inventory spreadsheet. Mae kissed the top of his head where a few strands of hair held fast.

"Wait, I need to finish this honey, hold on."

"You're still working? It's a beautiful Sunday afternoon, and you've already spent a whole week and most of the weekend working," she said. She walked to the sink and washed away the planter dirt from her hands.

"Mae I've told you before, it's all on me. If I don't take care of business, who will?" he said not looking away from his numbers.

"OK, I know this routine; I don't know why I fight it. Just tell me when you're available to talk, OK?" She walked passed him toward the kitchen doorway.

"OK, what's up?" Frank said looking up at his wife. Her cheeks were pink and glistening, and she had a cute smudge of dirt on her forehead.

"That was fast. What are you smiling at?" Mae asked putting one hand on her hip.

"Can't a man smile at his wife? Now, I'm all yours. What's up?" He knew that if he told his wife how beautiful he thought she was, smudge of dirt and all, she would not believe him.

"Well," Mae said pulling out a chair at the table to sit by Frank, "I went out to pick the tomatoes I've been watching and waiting to ripen, but there were none. They are all gone, just like that!" She snapped her fingers for effect. "I know it's not an animal because they at least leave some of the tomato behind ... with bite marks, but at least they leave something. Evidently, someone in our neighborhood thinks our garden is a salad bar."

"You know, if I had put the planters in the backyard we wouldn't have this problem," Frank countered distractedly.

"You know I don't like to work when that dog, Franz, is home alone. I'm afraid he'll come through the fence and maul me," Mae said half joking.

Frank looked at his wife. He had heard her, of course, but he had not really listened. The unfinished paperwork in front of him was distracting. During the week, he repaired appliances in people's homes, or worked in his showroom. So, he needed the weekend to catch up on bills and invoices.

It was this kind of work ethic that had kept Frank in business for thirty years and if he said so himself, he was a damn good repairman. He was not always his own boss though. Early in his marriage to Mae, he was employed by a successful repair company where he realized two important things.

The first thing he realized was that he had a knack for appliance repair. The second thing he realized was that he was paid much less than his bosses charged. Once he convinced himself he could create his own client base, he summoned the courage to go out on his own (with Mae's blessing of course). He never looked back.

He enjoyed his work so much, Mae saw it as a light load for him. She did not realize that for Frank, running the business was like swinging a bull over his head. If he took a break, or even slowed down, that bull would fall and crush him.

"Frank, you have that look in your eye," Mae said.

"Yes, I do. It's the look of problem solving … I am working on this tomato thievery situation in my head," Frank said, refocusing on the tomato dilemma. Mae smiled at her husband. Sometimes people underestimated Frank because he was a man of few words.

To know Frank, you had to observe him because he did not talk much about himself. Electric circuits were his specialty. One customer called him Doc after Dr. Frankenstein because he breathed life into inanimate objects. Another customer, an English teacher, thought Frank was aptly named because of his dry honesty.

Maybe he was so earnest because he took his responsibility so seriously. He had customers who trusted him with their homes. They gave him their house keys while they were away so they could return to working appliances. Frank staked the value of his business, and even his personal value, on being trustworthy.

Frank knew repairmen who would sell a brand new unit before they would clean your appliance, even if that was all it took to get it running like new. Frank's integrity may have cost him a little, but in the long run, at least he still had it.

"Mae, does this mean I'm not going to get anymore of your delicious homemade marinara sauce this year?" Frank asked, a look of mock fear in his eyes.

"That's right, Frank. Now you realize how serious this really is. I've got to do something soon. I've got big plans for those tomato plants! Maybe I should put a threatening sign in the planter."

"Won't that clash with your welcome mat?" Frank asked, raising an eyebrow.

"Good point."

"Let me finish up here and we'll figure something out, OK Mae? By the way, where's Lou? I haven't seen him around today." Frank reached for an invoice and opened a new window on his computer.

"He's at the library studying. He has finals next week." Mae reached for Frank's empty coffee mug and went to the sink with it. The sink was Mae's favorite part of the house because there was a wide window over it. From her sink, she could survey the canyon that surrounded their home.

"Summer break will be here soon. Does he have a job? Hey, I'm not done with that mug," Frank said.

Mae refilled Frank's mug with coffee from the carafe and returned the mug to him. Mae knew Lou's summer plans, but she kept silent about them. Anyway, Frank had become distracted by his paperwork.

She went back to the sink, and the view. Rooftops of neighborhood homes peaked through mature oak, pine, and eucalyptus trees. She traced where hidden roads wound around the canyon like ribbons. In the pale afternoon sky, she watched pairs of planes approach the airport until they descended passed her view. Everything in the view was so familiar, Mae's mind wandered freely.

Frank was right about summer, it was almost here. How many summers had she begun by reminiscing out this window? It seemed only yesterday she held Lou up in her arms so he could see this view, and now he was taller than she was.

Lou was their second son, though he was named after Louis, their first son. Louis, their first baby, had died during a traumatic birth. Mae's tormented grief over losing the baby she had carried to term was compounded by the fear she may never have another child. She and Frank were in their forties when he died.

Lou was born two years after his brother's death. His birth was a joyful consolation for both parents, but especially Mae, who found solace in her son's company. The shades of gray that had permeated her life since the death of her first child, developed into rich hues of color while she cared for her new baby. With Lou in his play pen, Mae transformed the yard she had let go to seed into a garden bursting with life.

How the seasons had flown! Her memories flipped through them like pages in a book. In the summer of Lou's second year, Mae planted a little apple tree in the middle of her backyard and every summer (until the next door neighbor's dog moved in) she notched a new mark in its trunk for Lou's stretching height.

She dressed Lou in warm sweaters and played "hide and seek" among the fat fall pumpkins. When the sun disappeared behind cloudy skies, Mae told Lou the sun hid its light inside the liquid yellow leaves of the autumn apple tree.

Mae and Lou's least favorite season was winter because they had to spend so much time indoors. They cheered each other with hot cocoa, and watched the rain from inside their cozy home. Sometimes, on those rainy days, they watched the raindrops make tracks down the window and guessed what Dad might be fixing at that moment.

Little Lou loved his father and wanted to be just like him. He imitated how Frank brushed his wavy hair out of his eyes with his pinky finger. Lou imitated his father's walk, talk, and even dress if Mae could find matching green shirts for him.

Like his father, Lou was fascinated by mechanics, and by making things work if they did not. From the moment he could hold a tool, Mae would discover gadgets in pieces on Lou's bedroom desk, or as Lou corrected, his "workbench." Now Mae could smile about finding "Jack" dislocated from his "Box." At ten years old, Lou had beheld the studded music drum he had extricated from his Jack-in-the-Box and exclaimed "Hey Mom, this one's just like the one I took out of your jewelry box!"

Lou was fascinated by how things worked and before he was sixteen he had unraveled the inner secrets of every electrical item in the house. Mae furthered his understanding by insisting he put the unraveled inner secrets back together again. Usually Lou reversed the process, and put everything back together, except the

17

time he cut open a battery with one of Mae's good steak knives.

"Remember when Lou rode his bike to the gas station to clean his cell phone with an air hose?" Mae asked, still looking out her window. Lou had learned Frank's mantra, "regular maintenance could keep things running indefinitely" but applied the lesson too enthusiastically. The force of the air hose cleared the cell phone of dirt and all of its innards too.

"Hmmm?" Frank's fingers were flying over the number pad on his keyboard. Mae regarded her preoccupied husband. When Lou was little, Frank's work schedule prevented them from spending a lot of time together. However, when Lou began to play football in high school, Frank found the time to watch his son play. Frank was a talented football player in his school days and Lou showed some of the same promise. He would go to all of Lou's games and occasionally a team practice. After the games, they reviewed every high and low, play by play.

Then, things changed. When Lou was in his second year of high school, he suffered two concussions from successive slam tackles. The doctor advised Lou to stop playing football or risk severe impairment. Ultimately, Frank and Mae could not risk the health of their only son; they knew the pain of losing a child. They pulled Lou off the team. Lou was disappointed but he accepted his fate graciously. He liked football but his end goal was repairing appliances, and working with his Dad.

Mae looked out of the window. She knew some day Lou would work with Frank in his appliance business, but when? And, why not this summer? After

18

all, Lou had almost finished his second year of college and he had a natural aptitude and desire for repair. She had to be subtle when dropping these hints on behalf of her appliance-smitten son. Lately Frank would shut her off like a blown fuse if she suggested a father and son team. Frank would say Lou was too young, too green, and too talkative to work with him. "I think better when things are quiet," Frank would argue.

Mae decided she should grease the wheel for Lou. "Frank, why don't you hire Lou for the summer?"

"Mae, we've been through this. You know I can't hire anybody. Do you remember what my papa used to say?"

Mae loved Frank's papa but he had said many clever things. "No, tell me, what did your papa used to say?"

"He used to say, 'when people are looking for a job, they are looking for work. When they find a job, they quit looking for work.' And I never forgot that! You can't measure how hard a guy will work when he starts making money!" Frank finished emphatically and saved a file on his computer.

"Oh Frank, you know what a hard worker Lou is. And you know he really wants to be a repairman," Mae chided. She thought of the many times Lou shadowed his father on weekend and evening emergency service calls. Mae loved the excitement in Lou's voice as he detailed every turn of his father's screwdriver. She did not understand why a father did not want his son to work with him.

It is not that Frank did not want his son to work with him. In fact, he liked having Lou around and he liked explaining repairs and pointing out the ins and outs of appliances. And though it was true that Frank liked to work in peace and quiet, there was another reason Frank had for not wanting Lou to work with him. It was something Frank could not tell his wife. At least, he could not tell her until the fall, or it would ruin his surprise.

Frank had plans. For thirty years he had worked every day of the week. They had postponed vacations, weekend, and holiday trips because of the business. Soon, they would have lots of time to be together. Frank had found a buyer for the shop. He planned to use the money from the sale for travel. He would take Mae to all of the places they fantasized about in the darkness of their bedroom before falling asleep. When they finished travelling, they would have money leftover to spend time in the woods (when Frank chose the destination), or on a tropical island (when Mae chose).

Frank had a plan for Lou too. Lou should get a college degree and work for a big business corporation after graduation. In a big company, Lou could work on weekdays and have time for his family on the weekend.

"Maybe Lou could apply for a job at one of the banks on Laurel Street," Frank suggested, hoping Mae would like the idea. She did not like the idea. She was doubtful Lou would like it either. Frank saw her expression and was grateful he could reveal his secret soon.

Two

LESSONS LEARNED

MONDAY MORNING, Frank drank the coffee Lou had made before he left for school. Frank considered himself an early riser, but Lou was always up first. Surprisingly, Mae was still in bed. Usually, they had breakfast together, but she would join him later in the showroom (Mae had been working at the shop since Lou was in high school and from home when he was little). Without thinking, he grabbed the sack lunch Mae had prepared for him from the fridge, found his briefcase next to the kitchen table, checked for his keys and left the house.

His service truck, the kind with multiple lockers in the bed for tool storage, was in the driveway. The sun was strengthening but the air was misty so he turned on his headlights and cruised down the winding roads to the bottom of the canyon. It was still early so he beat the commute traffic on the El Camino. El Camino Real was a fitting address for Frank's business because it means 'the Royal Road.' Frank liked to think of himself as the king of the repair business. He pulled into the back lot and parked next to his delivery truck.

He unlocked the back door, pivoted right into his office, and flipped on the lights. The bright fluorescent bulbs revealed a long white workbench which stretched the length of the office. Frank liked having his workbench close to his desk for convenience. On the wall behind the workbench hung a wide steel pegboard. Each tool that hung from the pegboard was outlined, labeled, and neatly arranged on pegs and shelves.

He removed the paperwork from his briefcase and set it on top of an old wooden desk in the middle of the room. He always prepped the desk before leaving work so every paper was in its place and the pencil cup was full of working pens and sharpened pencils. He loved this desk; it was his "mission control." An unmarked ink blotter protected it. A tower of stacked letter trays held neat piles of invoices, purchase and service orders. A black, streamlined phone sat at the corner of the desk within easy reach. A worn and comfortable leather desk chair beckoned its captain.

Frank prepared coffee at the little wet bar just inside the door, then he sat down at the desk. He organized the work from the weekend until he noticed something out of place. A sheet of white paper poked out from under the phone. It was a note from Lou that read 'Hi Dad, Mom said I could sweep up the shop and organize your toolbox while you were out on a repair. Have a good day.' It was another reminder that Lou wanted to work with him.

A twang of guilt pulled at Frank's heartstrings. Lou was pretty good at fixing appliances, and it was something he enjoyed. However, Lou needed his father. Frank could never leave Lou in business alone. There were too many pitfalls. For a fleeting moment he considered putting off retirement, and going into business with his son.

Anxiety quickly filled the void Frank's retirement plan left. Lou would need to understand that if he did not get paid, the business did not get paid. If the business did not get paid, they all went into the tank. The customer who taught Frank where the buck stops was one of his first customers after he went out on his own. Frank would always remember meeting her.

She had directed him to the rear of an otherwise empty garage, where her broken washer was, and left him to work. The washer needed a new pump so he replaced it, marked the bill 'paid,' and knocked on the back door. The woman opened the door, took the bill, and went inside to get a check, or so Frank thought. Frank cleaned up and waited, and waited.

Finally, he knocked on the door again. When the woman returned, he told her he needed to be on his way because he had other repairs and would she please pay him? She insisted he go on his way, with a piece of advice.

"If you mark your bills 'paid,' consider yourself paid." Without further adieu, she closed and bolted her door.

Frank was furious. He had marked the bill paid before she paid him but he could not prove it. The law was on her side. Tangling with the pathetic woman would be more trouble than the payment was worth. It was a tough lesson, one that he could spare his son if they went to work together. But what about the demands of owning a business? And, what about a life of perpetual overhead bull swinging?

He finished the last of his filing and looked at the framed photo of his papa hung by the door. Papa had owned his own deli. He had been a friendly, hardworking man. All of his customers loved him and his cooking. Though he worked every day of the week, he could not keep his potato salad stocked because his customers loved it so much.

That's when it hit Frank. He was doing the same thing to Lou that his father had tried, and failed to do with him. Frank's father had tried to discourage his son from owning *his* own business so he could put up his feet once in awhile and be home with his family on the weekends. When Frank told Papa he wanted to start his own appliance repair business, his father had said four words, "Give me your watch." Papa had been right about that. Frank's time was not his own since he started his own business.

However, Papa had been wrong about something else. Frank loved his life. While it was his responsibility to keep that bull swinging over his head, he was proud of the successful business he had built with his own hands. He was his own boss and he got to keep the profit, and the prestige that comes when you are a successful business owner. Every job, every dollar, every customer who recommended Frank, was the fruit of his talent, his knowledge, his effort. Frank loved his life because he could look at his success and say, 'I built that.' Should he deny his son that same satisfaction?

The coffee maker huffed and puffed its last drip into the carafe. Frank poured a mug full of the steaming black brew, and then stirred into it a teaspoon of sugar. The tempo of the day began with the metallic 'ting' of the spoon, the down beat for the telephone ring.

"Clean and Cold Appliances, Good Morning."

"Good morning, Frank? This is Jim's sister, Frances."

Frank tried to place her but the name did not ring a bell.

"We haven't met but you know my brother Jim, Jim Doyle?" she asked.

"Oh, sure, OK, you're Jim's sister. I haven't seen Jim in awhile, how's he doin'?" Frank asked.

"Fine, just fine, thanks. Listen, I was wondering if you could help me. My clothes washer isn't draining and I really let the laundry back up on me. Any chance you could help out the sister of an old friend this morning?"

Frank thought about it. Mae would be covering the shop soon, and Jim was an old friend. So, he should take care of the repair. He took down Frances' address, put his unfinished coffee in the little sink, and locked up the shop.

Frances lived just a few neighborhoods from the shop. She was chatty and friendly until she realized Frank wasn't listening. He was focused on replacing the bad pump on her washer and was never one to talk during a repair anyway. When he finished installing the new pump, he gave Frances the bill and gathered up his tools.

"This is so great, Frank. Thanks so much. I'm all out of checks but I ordered more last week. I should have the new ones soon. Can I mail the check to your office? I'm sorry to take advantage of our friendship, that way, but I'm good for it. I promise."

Frank was reluctant because he was not actually her friend, and because he had just been reminiscing about the pitfalls of customers, who took repairs for free. But what could he do?

"I don't usually do this Frances. My friends know if I don't get paid, I don't eat. Here's my card, just send the check to this address." He handed her his card. "And say hi to Jim for me, OK?"

"Sure thing! And don't worry, you'll get the check by next week. I promise," Frances said.

Three

NEW IN TOWN

ON THE OTHER SIDE of town, a loud blast from a train's horn heralded a stranger's arrival. Evelyn awoke before the train pulled into the San Elmos train station.

"Sequoiaaa Sta-aaa-tion!" the conductor announced over the intercom. Evelyn rubbed her eyes with the back of her bare, tattooed arm and grabbed a heavy backpack stuffed with her life's possessions. She stepped off the train and oriented herself. The sun had just set, but there was enough light to make out the landmarks her friend, Star, had described.

Evelyn felt badly that Star had stayed with Ricky, but it's a free country and everyone has a choice. With Ricky, the more money Evelyn made, the more he took. She had left home because she wanted more from her life. Now, she was eighteen, and she had taken enough from the slimy pimp.

She saved money by buying fewer drugs. The more money she saved, the more clear her thinking, and the more she wanted to leave Ricky. She squirreled her money away until she had enough to escape.

She had heard there were networks that would help, but she believed she could take care of herself and wanted no help from anybody.

It was dangerous keeping any cash from Ricky so the minute she thought she had saved enough, she left town. She could do better on her own, maybe in another business. She had been a cocktail waitress in Ricky's bars; maybe she could find work doing that again. The station lights were flashing to life and she realized it was too late to find an apartment. She needed to celebrate her liberation with a drink anyway. Evelyn had arrived.

Four

LINDA STRAISBURG

"HELLO?" Frank despised the little buttons on his cell phone. It annoyed him that to receive a call he had to press a 'send' button. This was just wrong. Frank believed it should say 'answer,' or even 'receive.' He also resented the tiny buttons. His fingers were too big for them and he often had to redial phone numbers if he hit two buttons at the same time. He waited uncertainly for the voice at the other end of the line to confirm he had actually answered the call.

"Frank?" Mae said.

"Yeah, it's me, you at the shop?" Frank asked.

"Yes I am. Thanks for making the coffee, Lou and I had some."

"Shouldn't Lou be looking for a summer job?"

"Frank, Linda called and she wants you up there right away," Mae answered, wanting to avoid the topic of Lou.

It worked. Frank forgot about Lou when he heard Linda Straisburg needed him. He had wanted to go back to the office for coffee with Mae. He had something to tell her, and he was looking forward to seeing her. However, he always chose work first.

"Did she say what she wanted?" Frank asked.

"Nope, short and sweet as usual," Mae answered. Frank grumbled his assent, hit the tiny "end" button on his cell phone and made a detour toward the freeway onramp. Highway 101 would be faster than El Camino and commute traffic was probably over. He did not like to keep Linda Straisburg waiting if he could help it.

Linda Straisburg capably managed a three building apartment complex in the town of San Nicholas. The apartments were luxurious and maintained impeccably by Linda. Professional tenants including pilots and flight attendants enjoyed the proximity of the airport. Other well to do tenants, including single doctors and nurses, lived in walking distance to a hospital.

Frank parked in the custodian parking space, and carried his toolbox down the path which wound through lush gardens in the buildings' courtyard. He knocked and let himself into Linda Straisburg's office which was off the courtyard near a decorative bird bath. She looked up from her French country table, which she used as a desk, and smiled warmly. She took off her reading glasses, stood, and reached out to Frank. He changed the hand holding his heavy toolbox so he could shake her limp hand.

"Frank, how nice you could come so quickly. I have a tenant in 332A whose garbage disposal has stopped working. I've filled out the time of your arrival on the work order, which I have here on my desk. The tenant is out for the day so let's be on our way, shall we? I'll let you into his apartment." Linda Straisburg picked up her voluminous key chain and led the way out of her office.

In all of the years Frank had worked for Linda, she never trusted him with a master key though her trust had grown in those years. Now, she let him into an apartment and left him alone to work. She reminded him often that this was a "unique privilege." No matter how long a repair took, other workmen were never left unsupervised in her tenants' apartments. He wished she would just give him a master key if she trusted him so much.

Frank followed Linda Straisburg silently down the richly carpeted hallway to the elevator. He observed that Linda's clothing, much like his own, rarely varied. Everyday he wore a clean green shirt and cargo pants, pressed the way he liked them by Mae. Linda Straisburg's uniform consisted of low black heels, a dark, tight fitting skirt, a white button down blouse, and sometimes a suit jacket if the weather was cool. She always wore a tasteful pair of diamond earrings which were visible because she swept back her dark hair into a clipped bun. She wore one gold bracelet on her right wrist, one plain gold watch on her left wrist, never a necklace, always a scarf. Her two carat diamond wedding ring was distracting but she did not flaunt it. It was given to her by her husband, twenty years her senior.

In the elevator Linda Straisburg said, "You know, I'm not sure what I should do. My husband is in the hospital. Nurses called twice this month urging me to visit immediately. Evidently, they thought he was on his death bed, but I knew better. He's fine. They don't understand I have pressing responsibilities," she said.

The elevator bell dinged at the third floor and the doors slid open sharply. They both stepped out of the

31

elevator. Linda continued around a corner, "they called again earlier today and again asked if I could rush over there. I mean, really, do they expect me to drop everything and rush over there?"

Frank stared at her, thinking she must be joking, but by the time he convinced himself she was not, she was knocking on the door of apartment 332A. "I've already phoned the apartment but I like to be doubly sure no one's home," she said. She took the master key, opened the door, and entered the apartment alone. Frank waited while she made extra, extra sure the tenant was not home. Finally, Linda invited him in.

"Thank you so much, Lou. I'll see you downstairs when you're done and then I'll give you the work order number," Linda Straisburg said while she sailing passed him toward the elevator. Evidently, the question about visiting her husband had been rhetorical because Frank had not had the opportunity to answer. For this, he was grateful.

Frank got down to his own business with the garbage disposal. He worked on it for forty-five minutes, an unusually long time for him. He ruled out many possibilities, but he did not find the source of the problem. Since he could not fix the disposal on site, he decided to replace it.

He planned to remove the broken garbage disposal first, then go the building's equipment closet for the new unit. At least Linda Straisburg had given him a key to the equipment closet door. However, once he left 332A, how would he get back in? He would have to track down Linda Straisburg to get back in.

Something about Linda Straisburg made Frank feel uncomfortable, though he never put his finger on it.

It seemed every word, every gesture, every dot to every 'i' was calculated for impact. What impact she wished to make was never clear to Frank.

He decided not to bother Linda, and instead planned to leave apartment 332A unlocked while he took the old garbage disposal to his truck. Then, he would get a new disposal from the equipment closet. He knew Linda would prefer the apartment door remained locked so he took the stairs to avoid seeing her.

All went according to plan. After he retrieved a new garbage disposal from the closet on the first floor, he took the stairs to the third floor. He let himself into the unlocked apartment and quickly installed the new unit. When he had cleaned up, he conscientiously locked the apartment door and took the elevator back down to the first floor. He would get the work order number from Linda Straisburg and he could be on his way. Linda Straisburg found Frank first.

"Frank! Frank! Come here, quick!" Linda Straisburg yelled from the end of the first floor hallway. Frank was shocked. He had never heard her voice at this volume or intensity. How could she have found out about him leaving the apartment door unlocked? His "unique privilege" of working in an apartment without her would surely be revoked. He never should have left the apartment unlocked, he thought, and he trudged down the hallway to take his medicine.

"Frank, you have to help us, come in," Linda said pulling him inside apartment 101A and closing the door behind him. A woman dressed in a sheer, black peignoir under a long, also sheer, black dressing gown sat in the living room. She held a tumbler of iced, amber colored liquid. Linda Straisburg's hair covered her

33

diamond earrings and her scarf had spun around so that the knot was at the back of her neck.

In a confident tone that belied her disheveled appearance, Linda Straisburg explained. "Frank, this is Ms. Peyton. She's had a rather unfortunate experience and we need your help. Ms. Peyton's neighbor dropped by for a visit and now he needs assistance getting back to his apartment."

"Sure, Linda, where is he? I'll help him back," Frank said, relieved he had not been observed leaving an apartment unlocked. He wanted to help the guy (who had probably had one too many), and leave quickly. Mrs. Peyton followed as Linda Straisburg led Frank to a bedroom where a decidedly dead, nude man lay on the bed, half draped in pink satin sheets.

"I was lucky to save myself he was so heavy," Ms Peyton said in scotch-scented breath.

"Linda, I'm not sure what you're asking me to do but I…" Frank stammered.

"Frank, this man's wife will expect him home when she returns from work this evening. We do not want to disappoint her, do we? Now let's each take an arm and bring him home," Linda Straisburg encouraged.

"I … I … I don't want to. This is not in my wheelhouse, Linda. I'm sorry but I have to leave." Frank left quickly but Linda Straisburg followed. She pleaded for his assistance and understanding. He ignored her and walked out of the building into the gardens.

Suddenly, something hit him on his shoulder. He turned to look at Linda Straisburg but she looked confused too. They both looked up at the same time to see a shower of ice rain down from the window of one floor to the balcony of the floor below it.

34

"Go ahead and call the police if you think the music is so loud!" the bearer of the ice bucket jeered at the now freezing woman beneath her.

"Never mind the work order, Linda, this one's on me," Frank called over his shoulder. He changed his gait to a jog on his way to the safety, and sanity of his truck.

Five

BICHO APARTMENTS

FRANK was never so happy to see Mae back at the shop. She was on the phone when he came in so he put the broken garbage disposal from Linda Straisburg's apartment on the work bench "to be fixed" area.

"Hey Pop," Lou said startling Frank.

"Hey, what are you doing here? I thought you'd be looking for a job," Frank said.

"Yeah, well, I've got to head up the hill, my last final starts in half an hour," Lou said. He kissed Mae on the cheek and left the shop. Mae finished her call.

"You would not believe the morning I just had, Mae. Linda wanted me to clear some dead guy out of his mistress's apartment, can you believe that?" Frank asked.

"What!? Mistress? Dead guy? How did he die?"

"I don't want to think about it, the woman was a little young for him…"

"I thought Linda was more careful about her tenants," Mae said primly.

"She is careful, when it comes to money. She runs a thorough credit check and if you're late on rent, you're out of there quicker than you can call your banker. You know what they say, money can't buy you

36

class... Oh, by the way, can you keep track of this bill? I put a new pump in Jim Doyle's sister's washer and she's going to send a check." Frank handed Mae the completed order.

"What, are we in the credit business now? I thought we agreed you'd get paid before you leave new customer jobs? Oh, Jay just called. He wants you over at the apartments to fix a blown fuse in the washroom again. *And* he has another job he said not to spend too much time on because the tenant is never happy anyway." She handed Jay's work orders to Frank.

After Linda Straisburg, Jay Bicho was Frank's biggest customer. Jay managed a large, flea bitten apartment building on Main Street for his younger brother, Bob Bicho. Bob was wealthy and owned several properties and businesses. Frank marveled at how a rich man like Bob Bicho (who had earned a fortune flipping homes in a hot real estate market) could sleep at night knowing his tenants lived in such squalid conditions. For that matter, why did a law student like his brother, Jay, not see the crime in mismanaging a building to the degree he did?

"Gee thanks. Thought I'd have a quiet afternoon but I guess that's not happening. I'll see you later Mae," he said.

"Hey, don't forget your lunch," she said handing him his sack lunch. Frank smiled, took the bag, kissed Mae's lips, and headed for the door. He'd need the strength so he ate while he drove the short distance south on El Camino. The morning at Linda Straisburg's apartments had been dramatic and any visit to the Bicho brothers' apartment could be its own theatre.

Growing up, the Bicho brothers had competed for the lead role. They were given the same privileges but different talents. The older of the two, Jay, went to private schools and made every teacher who taught him proud of their ability to teach. Jay had an excellent memory and a workhorse mentality. He relished his parents pride in him, and their disappointment in his little brother's lackluster grades. Ridiculing Bob's study habits was one of Jay's favorite stress relievers.

Jay grew older and went to larger schools where he encountered students with similar strengths and greater intellects, so his grades looked average. He earned his bachelor's degree with honors, and then considered whether to enter a working world where no grades would prejudice his value, or stay in his cocoon of academics. Ultimately, he concluded his superior debate skills (as exercised in his social circle) made him the perfect candidate for law school. Jay easily persuaded his father to fund the law school tuition.

Jay's younger brother, Bob, started in a private school but his grades embarrassed his teachers so they recommended he finish his education in public school. Bob showed talent in his high school wood shop and vocational classes but he found core academics boring and frustrating. When he studied for a test, it required a herculean effort to remember what seemed like mountains of written material. He narrowly graduated from high school, borrowed money from his Dad, and bought a charming, old bungalow in need of repair. Bob fixed the home to sell and earned a sizeable profit. He repaid his father and soon could buy several homes at once, remodel and sell them for attractive profits.

Bob's big brother, Jay, was not impressed with his little brother's labor intensive success, but he convinced Bob to let him manage one of his apartments, and live there rent free. The apartment was converted from a hotel built in the nineteenth century, into affordable housing units.

Jay viewed the tenants who lived in the apartments the way he viewed his brother. He could not possibly respect them because they lacked education and held menial jobs. He knew the government subsidized their rent but he never considered he too received help with his living. Instead, he felt it was his moral duty to make things a little difficult for his tenants. It motivated them, Jay reasoned, to strive for better living conditions elsewhere.

The Bicho apartments were located in the heart of downtown San Elmos. Downtown was a patchwork of vintage and contemporary. On his way to the Bichos, Frank drove by nineteenth century homes settled next to twenty-first century buildings. At a stop light, Frank admired a grand theatre constructed in 1928, turned right, and drove passed a multiplex of theatres housed in one, fluorescent illuminated, superstructure. Two blocks from Main Street he passed a stately, historic courthouse where he turned left and cruised by an imposing, multistory jail, and adjoining courthouse complex.

Frank marveled at how downtown San Elmos could change its scenery so quickly. Even the characters played diverse roles. The noon sun beamed down on a shoeless man pushing a stuffed shopping cart passed outdoor diners under colorful patio umbrellas. They were oblivious to each other, but not Frank who observed the spectacle.

"Who is it?" Jay called through the speaker in the grungy portico.

"It's Frank."

Jay buzzed the front door so Frank could get in, but he stayed in the comfort of his apartment. He preferred to avoid Frank when possible because he had misjudged Frank's intensity and integrity for conceit and arrogance.

Frank went into the laundry room and found the dryer that had shorted for the second time. He solved the problem by resetting the fuse. On his way to the next apartment repair, he pondered the problem of the fuse. Why would one dryer on one circuit blow a fuse?

The fuse issue was still bothering him when he knocked on the door of apartment 204. A woman opened the door, her little girl beside her. Sometimes kids were shy, so to put the child at ease, Frank smiled broadly. The little girl showed no expression and would not look at Frank. Her mother, however, was vivacious and friendly. She wore jeans and a Giants baseball team t-shirt. Frank followed the pair into the kitchen while Mom explained the problem.

"There's a 'whir' sound that starts up, and then the whir sound stops with a 'clang.' I never would have noticed it but my daughter is autistic and her hearing is very sensitive."

Lou looked at the girl and he wondered, with her blank expression, if she knew they were talking about her. Her mother seemed to understand because she said, "Don't worry, she's in there. You've heard the expression 'still waters run deep'? Well Julia understands everything going on around her, she just can't express her recognition the way we can." Just then, the fan on the refrigerator turned off and Frank heard the 'clang.' Julia ran out of the room.

"You see? It really bothers her. Jay doesn't understand autism. He thought I was spoiling her by worrying about a little noise in the refrigerator. I reminded him four times to call someone to fix it. I didn't like bothering him but it's been upsetting Julia for months…"

"I wish I could have done something sooner. Julia seems like a young lady who has a lot of thinking to do and I don't like distractions when I'm thinking either," Frank said. He went to work quickly and placed some felt pads under the defrost pan which would absorb the clanking sound. Julia's mother was grateful.

"Thank you so much for understanding. It might be a small repair for you, but it means a lot to us." They deserved all the help he could offer, but Frank could do nothing if Jay did not ask him. One of these days, Jay would get on his last nerve for how he treated his tenants. He would retire soon. He hoped his nerves could last until then.

Six

A PLACE TO CALL HOME

IT WAS THE LAST TIME, she promised herself. Evelyn got out of her host's apartment before he woke, and found a nearby gas station with an unlocked restroom in which to wash. Inside, the walls were grimy and wet paper towels lined the floor.

She looked at her reflection and rationalized her lapse in progress. The bar was closing, and she had no where to go. She had had no choice but to spend the night with that man, whatever his name was. The guilt she felt over pinching money from his wallet would pass. She felt worse about her alcohol intake. Her stomach threatened to cramp and expel what little it contained. She was proud she had spent none of her own money, and she had refused several offers to get high. All things considered, she did the best she could.

She left the dark restroom, renewed by the bright morning sun and the cool air on her face. Her friend had given her the address of an apartment building nearby. The rooms were small and expensive, but vacancies were scarce. On Main Street, she passed 'The Coffee Shop' and saw her reflection in its large tinted window. She admired her large and imposing silhouette created by the giant backpack she wore.

Then her gaze went beyond her reflection to the room inside. She cupped her hands like horse blinders on the window, and surveyed the interior. This was no coffee shop. Black, leather-top stools lined a long, dark wooden bar. Around the tables which dotted the old plank floor were hard back chairs. Two of the chairs lay on their backs like tipped cows. It was a good omen to find potential employment so close to a potential apartment.

Walking further down the street, she found the address which matched the one scrawled on the inside of a matchbook by her friend. She pressed the manager doorbell.

"Yeah?" Jay answered sleepily.

"I'm looking for an apartment."

"Do you have $1000 cash for first and last?"

"Yes."

Evelyn had forgotten about the deposit. Employment would be her next priority if she was going to make next month's rent.

Seven

WIVES

FRANK got home late. After he finished at the Bicho place, he had a special mission to accomplish at his shop. Mission accomplished, he arrived home at dusk to find his house dark. He called through the house for Mae. The hall light switched on and Mae padded out of their bedroom with tousled hair and drowsy eyes.

"Mae, can you come in the kitchen please? I want to talk to you." Frank switched on the kitchen light and sniffed the dinner Mae had left on the counter for him. He grabbed a fork and took the plate to the table. Mae came into the kitchen but she did not say anything. Instead, she went to the cupboard for a glass. She filled it with water from the tap, thirstily emptied it, and then refilled her glass.

"The meatloaf is delicious Mae, thanks. Guess what? You know that tomato problem you're having? Well, I think I may have solved it. I figured out how to scare anyone from taking your tomatoes, without being rude. Take a look by the front door." He gestured with his thumb toward the door and took a forkful of mashed potatoes. Silently, Mae put the glass down and walked to the entry where she saw a placard on a stick. It read, 'Public Notice: Testing Chemicals.'

"All we have to do is put the sign in the planter and I think soon enough we'll be eating marinara again. You'd have to be pretty desperate to steal a tomato that's been sprayed with chemicals! What do you think?" Still at the table, he put a forkful of peas into his mouth. He waited, but Mae did not respond. From behind, he heard an ominous thud on the tile floor. He pushed back his chair and hurried to the entryway. Mae had collapsed onto the floor. She was conscious but cold and clammy and her breaths were shallow.

"Mae, what's happened, what's wrong?"

"I really fell for your sign, Frank." She managed a smile but Frank was stern.

"What's going on Mae?"

"I'm not sure... I've been feeling so tired lately. I can't sleep with my heartburn. Just help me up, I'll be OK."

Just then, Lou let himself into the house. He was startled by the sight of his father kneeling over his mother on the floor. He hoped the sign in his mother's grip was no indication of the problem.

"What's going on you two?" he asked.

"Lou, your mother collapsed. Help me get her in the truck; we're taking her to the hospital. Don't even think about arguing, Mae."

"Well, at least put the warning sign in the tomato bed first," Mae said.

⌛

The next morning, Frank woke up alone in his bed. He looked at the pillow where his wife's head usually rested and thought of her alone in her hospital room. The doctor had said it was probably just over exertion, but they wanted to keep her overnight for observation and to check some anomalies in her EKG. Frank readied himself for work quickly, saving time by not shaving. Lou was already in the kitchen sipping hot coffee when Frank entered.

"What are you doing today?" Frank asked.

"Well, I finished my finals so I'm on summer vacation," Lou answered.

"Why don't you stay home and clean up so your Mom can come home to a nice house," Frank said. He decided to skip breakfast and grabbed the keys to go.

"Uh, Dad, I thought I could come in to work with you today," Lou said.

"Uh… Listen, Lou. I think your Mother would appreciate seeing you. Why don't you go by to see her after you clean up here? OK? That's a good kid, I gotta go, see you after work," Frank said rushing out the door.

Frank felt guilty for not taking Lou along but suddenly his plan to retire became urgent. Mae's sudden collapse reminded him no one's future is guaranteed. Frank was more determined than ever to use the time they had left fulfilling their lifelong plans.

He wanted to see Mae, but first he had an important and fabulously wealthy customer to visit. Impressing this customer might assure an early retirement.

The client's address was on Alameda Avenue, a tree lined but somewhat busy street. The house, however, was separated from the avenue by an ivied wall, a small grove of redwoods, and a large lawn. To get on the property Frank's service truck had to be admitted remotely through a wide swinging gate.

A tall and muscular butler let Frank in the house. Another burly gentleman, dressed in an island floral resort shirt, led him to a kitchen that was too small for the home. Though he had not seen him for years, Frank thought he recognized the big man sitting in the little breakfast nook off the kitchen. Perhaps he was mistaken. The customer had provided a different name than the one he remembered.

"Eddie? Is that you? How are you?" Frank said reaching his hand out.

"Frank, I am very happy to see you, it has been a long time. How are you, how is life treating you? Would you like a cup of coffee, or juice perhaps?" Eddie asked.

A tall, voluptuous, blond wearing a bathing suit under a sheer pool coat breezed barefoot into the kitchen. "Oh! Thank you for coming! It will be so good to get this trash compactor going again!" she said with a look of sincere gratitude.

"Frank, this is my beautiful wife, Kerry. Kerry, this is my old friend from high school, Frank. We used to play football together."

"Isn't this a small world? I'm very pleased to meet you, Frank." She smiled sweetly and went out the back door. Eddie watched her leave and went back to the paper he was reading.

"I'll just get started on the trash compactor here," Frank said. Eddie seemed to have forgotten Frank but it did not matter, Frank was already checking the compactor. He removed an obstruction which got the trash compactor online again. Frank was writing up the bill when Kerry came back into the kitchen.

"You're finished! I have such perfect timing I can't believe myself sometimes," she said. "I'll get the

47

checkbook." She walked gracefully to an alcove off the kitchen and opened a drawer from which she took a leather bound binder of checks.

"I will pay the bill," Eddie said. Kerry looked surprised.

"But Eddie, I always pay the bills," she said, disappointed he would deprive her of this small joy. Eddie's expression did not change so she shrugged and brought the check binder to him. She took a sip of his coffee, and went back outside. Eddie took the bill from Frank and asked,

"Do you want me to tell you why I am paying the bill, Frank? I am paying the bill because I ordered a patio table, chairs, and three loungers from a store that is downtown. I paid cash for the furniture, in full. When the furniture was delivered to my home, my wife signed for the delivery and gave a check to the delivery man for the cost of the furniture, again. Subsequently, when the furniture store sent a receipt for the payments that had been made by my wife *and* by me, she mailed them another check for the amount that we had together already paid them. Frank, you know, I've got a lot of money. I probably could have a lot more if I had been paying the bills all this time of my marriage." Eddie finished writing the check and tore it from its sheet. He handed the check to Frank.

"It was certainly very nice to see an old friend. Thank you for your service, we will call you again. Is there anything I can do for you, Frank? Please do not hesitate to ask an old friend." Eddie reached out his hand and grabbed Frank's in a warm grip which he did not release until Frank answered,

48

"Uh, no, thank you very much Eddie, I'm fine, but it was great seeing you again."

"Bobby, Frank, my friend, is leaving now." Eddie let go of Frank's hand and Bobby, the "escort," appeared. His sudden appearance unnerved Frank and he followed nervously behind the burly man to the entryway where the butler opened the door. His phone chirped and for once Frank was grateful to have his phone ring.

"Hello?"

"Frank, this is Jay. I've got a couple of problems over here. First off, that dryer blew a fuse again. Second, I need to get rid of a refrigerator."

"The dryer again? I can't figure out why it keeps blowing. Anyway, don't worry; I'll take care of the fuse and the fridge today."

"Yes, not tomorrow, today," Jay said petulantly. Frank pushed the 'end' button carefully. When he got inside his truck, he punched the phone number of an old friend, Exelda, into his phone.

Eight

EXELDA

FRANK listened to the phone ring on the other end of his cell phone line. He had known Exelda since the early days of his business. In those days, he would unpack his inventory of new appliances in the back lot and stack the broken down cardboard in piles.

One day on the back lot, Frank was loading his truck for a trip to the dump when Exelda pulled into his driveway in a little Chevy Luv pick up. The truck was loaded like a Jenga tower with tenuous ropes strapping two refrigerators and one washer to the tiny bed. The little truck listed from side to side until it came to a stop in front of the stunned repairman.

"Hello there," Exelda had greeted him from her driver's window. Lamar, an older man, sat in the passenger seat and did not acknowledge Frank. Lamar did not trust most people and he did not feel comfortable in certain neighborhoods. Frank was wary too until he saw the sign on the side of the truck, "Excellent Hauling, East Los Alto, Call Anytime"

"Hi, what can I do you for?" Frank asked.

"Well, I'd like to make you a proposition. I'm Exelda White, and this is my uncle, Lamar White. We have a hauling and scrap business together. We'll haul anything you got at no charge. We make our money selling the metal and cardboard," she said.

Frank smiled at her open style and looked over at his lot. Old appliances and empty cartons were lined up, ready to be loaded and taken to the dump. He would have to close the shop to make the trip, and he'd have to pay the dump to take the haul. Not only that, if he did not remove the cartons right away, the kids in the neighborhood would steal them.

He did not have a problem with the kids at first. He knew they used the cardboard as sleds to skim down dirt hills. It was when the police questioned him about illegal dumping of his appliance boxes at the bottom of those dirt hills that he had a problem with the kids.

Frank reached out his hand and introduced himself. Exelda pumped his hand and smiled. Then, Frank reached out his hand to Lamar. For one awkward moment, it looked as if Lamar would shun Frank's friendly gesture. Then, Lamar slowly stretched his hand out and clasped Frank's. They shook quickly, and Lamar looked away again.

Exelda picked up the phone.

"Hello?"

"Hey Exelda, this is Frank."

"Hey Frank, how you doin'?" Exelda asked.

"Fine. Fine, you know. How's Lamar?"

"Ornery, just like always! How's Mae?"

"Well, not so good, Exelda. We had to take her into the hospital yesterday with breathing problems... don't worry, they say she's fine, just watching her to be sure."

"Frank, that's too bad. If I know Mae, she's going crazy in a hospital bed. She'd rather be taking care of someone or something."

"She hates it but she's probably still taking care of someone. She's probably getting the nurses' email addresses so she can send recipes to 'em." They both laughed. Frank got down to business.

"Jay Bicho's got a refrigerator he needs taken away; can you pick it up, Exelda? He said it would be in the lobby."

"Sure thing, Frank, we'll get right over there. Say hello to Mae for me would you? I hope she feels better real soon."

"Will do, Exelda, thanks. Maybe we'll see each other at the apartment; Jay's got a job for me too."

"Sounds good Frank, see you later," Exelda said and hung up. It was always good to hear from Frank. Exelda had known him for almost twenty-five years so they had seen each other's ups and downs. She was there when he lost his first baby son and when Lou was born.

Frank knew her story too. He knew her when she graduated from college, lived on her own for a few years, and worked for the County Clerk's Office when she was not helping her mother's brother Lamar on the weekends. She remembered meeting Frank all those years ago after she had encouraged Lamar to branch out to new customers. Lamar liked the idea of growing his business, but meeting new people, especially white people, made him queasy.

Lamar was a kind man but he had a streak of racism that rarely reared its head. He justified his prejudice because of the racist insults hurled at him by white strangers walking by him in the street or driving by him in their cars.

Exelda learned of this tendency in her otherwise loving uncle when she was a child. Lamar was visiting the same day Exelda had a little white guest over to play. He took it upon himself to serve a snack to the pair of little girls. He gave her white friend a snack of saltine crackers on a pie tin and he handed Exelda a snack of cheese, crackers, and fruit on a china plate.

"Uncle Lamar! We've got to head over to the Bicho apartments to pick up a fridge, you ready to go now?"

"Girl, why you always shoutin'? I'm ready, I'm always ready. Look, I got my keys right in my hand. Now I'm more ready than you!" he said.

Exelda laughed and ran to the front door. "Guess I beat you out the front door Uncle!" she teased. Lamar chuckled and jogged after her.

Nine

THE WELCOME COMMITTEE

IT'S NOT THAT EVELYN had never encountered a pistol, she had many times. It was just that she did not expect to hear one shot so soon after arriving at her new apartment. She peaked out her door in time to see a the back of a man running toward the stairwell.

"You damn fool, you almost shot me! Your own mother!" a woman shouted from her open apartment door.

"Next time, give me the money, you bitch," her son threatened before he disappeared down the stairs.

"Feels like home already," Evelyn thought as she closed her door. She took a look around her new apartment. A thousand dollars did not buy much, she concluded, but home was home. The kitchen was small but she twirled in it, feeling like a princess. A light blue recliner chair was the only furniture in the small studio apartment. She looked out of its one window and absorbed the view of the parking lot behind the apartment. The only greenery was a tree below her window.

A knock at the door startled her. She wanted to meet her neighbors but she felt unprepared. She opened the door anyway.

"Surprise!"

"Ricky!" Evelyn said, shocked. He pushed her so hard into the apartment she lost her balance and tripped backward over the back pack she had left on the floor. Ricky shut the door behind him and knelt on Evelyn's chest.

"You don't look happy to see me, what's wrong?"

"How did you find me?"

"A mutual friend, who, by the way, did not want to get stuck with your loan payment."

"Ricky, I paid you back everything I owe you," Evelyn said. Ricky pinched her cheeks together with one of his hands and pointed at her with his other.

"I thought you were my girl. I thought you knew you were my girl. You're not done with me until I say so."

He got up and looked around the studio.

"Evelyn, you're so stupid and yet this is working out perfect. Do you know that you got this apartment because of me? Jay is like a brother to me. He let you stay here because of me. Now you be good to my friends and I'll be back next week to collect my due. Don't cross me again, Evy, my girl." He rolled her off her backpack and unzipped the front pocket where Evelyn had stored her first month's rent.

"Evelyn, too much cash makes a girl lazy."

Ten

DAR

ON THE DRIVE to the Bicho apartment, Frank startled himself remembering Mae was in the hospital. Frank could always feel her on his heart but his mind was free to take care of business knowing she would take care of everything else. This new, unfamiliar concern stuck in his throat and threatened to overwhelm him. He drove quickly to Dar's jewelry shop, just two blocks from the Bicho apartments.

Dar was originally from India. His father had emigrated from India with his wife and only child, Dar. When Dar was a teenager, his Dad died suddenly after a heart attack. Dar inherited his father's jewelry business, quit school and ran the shop with his mother until she too died leaving Dar alone except for family back in India.

Frank found a parking space across from Dar's shop and darted through traffic across the street. He walked by the display windows in front of the shop that held sparkling rings, necklaces, and watches and pushed open the glass, store door. Two display cases flanked the red carpet that led to the front where a wide case displayed the largest and most expensive pieces.

"Hey Dar? It's me, Frank," Frank announced to the empty showroom. Dar came out of the backroom, his smile lighting up his brown eyes.

"Frank, my friend, how good to see you! Where is my coffee?" He smiled.

Frank laughed and said, "No coffee today, my friend. I am on an errand of mercy. Mae is in the hospital," Frank said.

"Mae?! What happened, is she OK?"

"Oh, I think she's fine. The doctors think that maybe it's just over exertion. They say she needs to rest, but I thought that maybe you might have something to cheer her up. What looks good today?"

Dar knew when to pump his old friend for information and when to proceed cautiously. Frank was uncharacteristically light hearted and care free which meant his heart must be very heavy.

"Frank, I have the perfect gift. My man just delivered it. It's a diamond ring with sapphires that will match the diamond and sapphire earrings you bought Mae at Christmas. Here, let me show you." Dar retrieved a felt covered drawer from behind the counter which framed the sparkling gemstones. He had prepared the presentation knowing he'd see Frank eventually.

"That looks pretty good, she'll like that one. I'll take it. Here's my credit card. I've got to go down to the Bichos, any news in the neighborhood?"

"Oh yes, my friend. You know the little coffee shop down the street? I think I met my future wife there. It has turned topless," Dar said running Frank's credit card through the scanner. He looked through his spectacles at the keypad, punched a few numbers, and then returned the card to Frank. He put the diamond ring into a white jewelry box and snapped it shut.

"Dar, I don't know how to tell you this but that's not a coffee shop, it's a bar."

"I had suspected this, my friend. The coffee is not very good," Dar said while tilting his head for emphasis.

"They can't go topless can they? The police won't let them."

"Well, my friend," Dar said scratching the few hairs left on his freckled head, "maybe the police don't know about it yet, maybe they do, please sign here." He held out a pen for Frank who signed the receipt, took his copy, and put ring box into his pocket.

"Hmmm. Well, be sure we get an invite to the wedding, Dar. I'll see you; I've got to fix a fuse before Jay blows his. Next time I'll bring coffee so you don't have to go looking for it," Frank said with a wink.

"Good bye my friend, extra sugar next time, good bye!"

Dar was the best jeweler Frank knew and this was partly why they were friends. Dar sold good quality merchandise at a fair price and to Frank, you could tell a lot about a person who ran their business honestly. He was a man Frank could trust and the feeling was mutual. Sometimes Frank stopped by Dar's shop with two cups of coffee (the stronger the better), and they would discuss everything from business to personal concerns. They solved the problems of the world and made up some of their own. Their political views often matched, but they never could agree on the best baseball team.

Frank bought a lot of jewelry from Dar. Mae loved jewelry and she knew the gifts expressed the feelings Frank's words could not. Some of Mae's friends from the Garden Club suspected the quantity of jewelry she received from her husband. One lady brazenly suggested to Mae (what others in her circle were thinking) that Frank must be compensating for guilt he felt over affairs. Mae ignored the suggestion and wore her jewelry proudly. The thrill some people found digging in the dirt only made Mae want to soar higher above them.

Frank had parked his truck a few blocks from the Bichos apartment but he decided it would be better to move the truck closer in case he needed something from it. It took awhile before he found another parking space because he wanted to leave the loading zone open for Exelda. The only space he found was a few blocks in the opposite direction so, in the end, he had not moved the truck any closer. By the time he arrived at the Bicho apartment, Lamar and Exelda had parked in the loading zone and were getting out of their truck. After Jay buzzed them all in, they discovered two men struggling with a small refrigerator in the apartment stairwell.

"Here, let me help," Frank offered. He and Lamar helped guide the heavy appliance into the lobby.

"OK, break it up. Frank, I'm not paying you to haul appliances, I need you to fix 'em, follow me," Jay demanded on his way through the lobby, toward the laundry room.

Exelda and Lamar observed Frank. He remained calm by remembering something he had heard Mae say, "that's his choice; I would make a different one." Frank chose his words carefully. He followed Jay into the laundry room.

"Jay, I'm happy to work for you, but I don't like being ordered around, you know?" Frank said.

Jay suddenly felt very alone with just him and Frank in the laundry room.

"Oh I am so sorry, Frank. I don't know what got into me. I've been under so much stress lately, I... I..." Jay stammered, all of his bravado evaporating. Satisfied his message had been received, Frank turned to the business at hand.

"I can't figure out why this fuse keeps blowing, Jay. There's only one dryer on the outlet..."

"That's why you get paid the big bucks, Frank, just fix it." He squeezed by Frank and exited the back door of the laundry room. Frank sighed and knelt down in front of the outlet again. This time, he decided to take a look behind the plug plate. That's where he discovered a hole drilled underneath the outlet. He followed a wire connected to the outlet which ran through the hole disappearing somewhere behind the wall.

He knelt with his head almost to the floor to peak through the hole. Shocked by his discovery, he stood up again. He would have to wait until he saw Jay to tell him he had solved the case of the blown fuse. First, he had to fix a refrigerator upstairs.

"Excuse me, Mr. Frank?" The two men who had just hauled the refrigerator down the apartment stairs stood in the doorway. Frank could see Exelda and Lamar behind them in the hall.

"Yes, what can I do for you?"

"Mr. Frank, we have a problem. Mr. Jay no pay us for the jobs we did today."

"Did he say he would pay you?"

"Yes, he no say how much but yes, he say he pay both of us for working for him today."

Frank finally understood another puzzle that had nagged him. Jay never sent the same men to Frank's shop for deliveries. This was curious because they seemed like pretty good workers and nice guys you would hire again. Now Frank understood what was going on. Jay considered the quantities of willing workers standing at strategic intersections, his own personal orchard of free labor for the picking. He got a new crop of men before he had to pay the last crop.

"I didn't realize. If I can help, I will," Frank said. He felt sorry for the men but he would not be able to do anything for them right then. He had to finish a job for Jay in apartment 144 so he could visit Mae.

Three months before, Frank installed a new refrigerator in apartment 144. Jay bought the snowball type of freezer which needs defrosting every few months. They were inexpensive refrigerators, but the tenants did not like them because of the extra maintenance they required.

"Appliance Man," Frank announced to the man on the other side of the door. The door flew open to reveal a slim young man in a Bob Marley t-shirt. His was in training for dread locks but was still in the 'bed head' phase. He let Frank in and waved his arm dramatically at the refrigerator. Frank took one sniff of the air and diagnosed the problem.

"This refrigerator you put in here is no good, man. Nothing stays cold. My milk's bad; my ice cream is melted. It's not cool, man, I'm telling you. You gotta get me a new one, man."

"OK, I hear you, but do you remember when I installed it for you? I told you how to defrost your freezer, remember? I told you to turn off the controls, and keep an eye on the drip pan while the ice melts. You can't get impatient with these freezers and start whacking away at the ice."

"Yeah, man, I did that man, but that's not the problem. The freezer's not cold, that's the problem, man."

"If it's not cold, why did you need to defrost it?" To test his suspicion, Frank found the hole he had expected to find on the evaporator tube. "How did this hole get here?" he asked.

"I don't know, man."

"Well, then let me tell you how I think it got there. Your refrigerator has worked perfectly for three months, which is why you have not complained about it not being cold until now. Three months is about the length of time it takes before you have to defrost these freezers. You were in a hurry, so you used something sharp to scrape the ice out. That's how you poked a hole in the evaporator tube. When I came into the apartment, I smelled the burning oil. The little smell told me there was a hole and your compressor had gotten overheated."

"Wow, are you a detective, man?"

Frank was flattered but stayed with the matter at hand. "Look, I don't want to leave you without a fridge. I'll get you a loaner but you have to promise me you'll take care of it."

"It's a deal, thanks man, I'll let the ice melt natural next time, I promise on my honor, man."

⧗

By the time Frank dropped off the loaner refrigerator it was late and he did not want Mae to wonder what had happened to him. He hopped down the stairs, two by two, to the lobby.

"Frank!" Jay called out before Frank's fingers could get a hold of the front door knob, "did you take care of that refrigerator in 144 I told you to fix?"

Frank kept his cool. "Jay I needed to bring it back to the shop to fix it so I just dropped off a loaner refer for the guy in 144. I'm in a hurry so I'll talk to you …"

"Oh, you're in a hurry are you? Frank, I ask you to do one thing, fix a refrigerator and it's still not done?"

Frank paused, then answered calmly, "That's right, Jay. It's not fixed yet. I'll let you know when it's done. Oh, I meant to tell you, I figured out why that fuse keeps blowing in the washroom. The guy in the next door apartment is using that laundry room plug to run his personal appliances. He was pretty clever about it; the connection wire was hidden under the plug plate."

Jay blanched but recovered quickly, "I still don't get the connection; why does the fuse blow?" Jay asked.

"Well, the fuse blows when one of the appliances in his apartment is on at the same time the dryer in the laundry room is on. The fuse can't handle all of those appliances on the same plug." He paused and observed Jay's reaction. "I thought you'd be more upset about one of your tenants taking advantage of you like that," Frank said.

"Oh… Well, I am very upset about it but it's my problem, Frank. I'll take care of it. Don't you worry about it. Yeah. Well, I'm busy so, I gotta go. Remember, fix that refrigerator, Frank." Jay turned to go.

"Jay, I know it is your apartment on the other side of the laundry room. I know you drilled the hole, and that you make the fuse blow, and that you make me come out here every damn time it does. I also know you've been using workers like toilet paper. If you stiff one more man who works for you, I'll tell your brother what you've been doing with the electricity."

Jay did not care if his brother found out about his little "electric share" situation, but it was better if his brother's attention was diverted elsewhere in case other matters were exposed.

"Are you accusing me of something, Frank? Or are you just threatening me?"

"Cut the crap, Jay. It's time you started treating people decently and I'll be your worse enemy until you do."

Jay was silent but recovered. "I let those people stay in my apartment, and they do a little work for me. So what?"

"Yeah. So what? That's probably what your brother will say too. Should I ask him?"

Jay's face turned red. Frank had never crossed him like this. Jay pitied the man who crossed him.

"I don't see any reason to bother my little brother about this. I had intended to pay those men and I'm insulted they've accused me unjustly before I could pay them. You wouldn't understand, Frank, but I'm a busy man. I get a lot done; it just takes a little longer. Well, I'd love to stay and chat some more, but like I said, I'm a busy man." He turned and practically ran out of the front door with no protest from Frank.

The traffic on the way to the hospital was light but it did not help Frank's mood. If he had not discovered the hidden wire, how many more times would Jay have called him about that fuse? He had ignored the inconvenience of going out of his way for such a small job because Frank appreciated Jay's long standing partnership.

It was maddening to discover Jay cared less about Frank's time, than the dollars he saved from his monthly utilities. Frank consoled himself with more words of Mae, 'it was a small percentage of people who made bad choices.' He could not wait to see her.

Eleven

HOME IS WHERE THE HEART IS

FIRST, Frank stopped by the grocery store to pick up a bouquet of flowers for Mae, then he drove to Sequoia hospital. Both of their sons were born there. The memories the hospital provoked sent shivers up his spine.

He walked through the bustling lobby and caught an 'up' elevator before the doors closed. Mae's room was to the right of the seventh floor elevators, opposite the maternity wing.

"Hey, aren't you supposed to be in bed?" Frank asked, surprised to see Mae out of her hospital gown, dressed, and ready to go.

"The doctor came by this morning, I've been discharged! Let's go," she said. She grabbed her overnight bag, the flowers, and a kiss on Frank's cheek on her way out. Frank caught up with her at the elevators.

No one would recognize them as the same couple who waited there for an elevator, twenty five years before, with heavy hearts while their first born son lay swaddled in the hospital morgue. The green 'down' triangle dinged and the elevator doors slid open.

Sad memories filled their silent descent. Frank remembered he could not console his wife over the death of their first child, but he could immerse himself in the ovens, washers, and refrigerators of his loyal customers. He could fix appliances. If one died or broke, he restored it. If he could not fix it, he replaced it. The hardest part of those days was that he could not fix the person he loved most, his Mae.

He sublimated his powerlessness into work. He worked long hours, received glowing recommendations and in those days of grief, business thrived. When Mae became pregnant with their second son, hope again breathed into their lives. Hope they felt twenty years before in the same elevator. Putting his memories aside, Frank winked at Mae. The elevator doors slid open and they stepped into the lobby.

Lou was surprised to see his mother walk through the front door. He had finished cleaning up the house and was about to go visit her in the hospital. He gave his Mom a big hug and a long look. "Well, Mom, they let you out. I guess that means you're OK?"

"I am fine, I promise. I'm glad to see you." She pinched his cheeks softly and hugged him tightly. The men strongly suggested she rest but Mae soldiered passed them to her bedroom. She unpacked her overnight bag and stored it in her bedroom closet. Again, the men watched helplessly while she marched by them on her way to check her tomato plants.

"Eureka!" she called from the front yard. She stepped into the house triumphantly holding one tomato in the air with one hand, and a basket full of ripe tomatoes in the other.

"I guess no one wanted to test our chemicals! Frank, you are a genius." The hug and big kiss she gave Frank made both him and Lou blush. She let go of her husband and marched into the kitchen where she turned on the oven for baking, then began pulling out pots, the food processor, olive oil, garlic…

"Hey, what do you think you're doing young lady? You just got home from the hospital. Don't you think you should take it easy?" Frank asked. Mae ignored his and Lou's protests and began preparing her famous, and delicious, marinara sauce for a pasta dinner.

Lou was relieved to have his Mom home. The air seemed lighter and she improved his Dad's mood too. He sat down at the kitchen table, which for once was not covered with paperwork.

"Frank, do you remember in the old days the funny ways you sometimes got paid?" Mae asked between bursts of the food processor. The tomatoes whizzed around in a red whirl.

"Which time do you mean? People were pretty creative back then," Frank smiled and sat at the table too.

"Lou, your father was just too nice in the old days. Word spread in the country part of town about how nice he was. He worked for these darling, little old ladies who could explain clearly what was wrong with their stove or their dryer but when it came to paying the bill? They would forget how to speak English!" Mae laughed and Lou chuckled.

"So they didn't pay you?" Lou asked.

"They'd pay me with a jar of pesto or marinara… never as good as your mother's, I might add. Those jobs were worth at least ten jars of your mother's

68

sauce!" Frank smiled at the memory. "Lou, I want you to think about this. If you start your own business, sometimes you have to make sacrifices and do jobs you think are beneath you. I remember one of my first jobs. This guy brought me into his kitchen, right? I say, 'So what's the problem?' He says, 'It's the broiler.' I say, 'Yeah? What's wrong with it, is it not heating?' He says, 'No, it works.' I say, 'OK.' He says, 'It's dirty.' I say, 'It's dirty?' He says 'Yeah.' Well, like I said, I'm hungry for business and I can't be choosy. I got bills to pay! So I told him to wait a minute, I'd be right back. I went to the supermarket and bought oven cleaner. I cleaned that oven spotless. I knew how to take that oven apart and put it back together with my eyes closed, but that's not what he was going to pay me for. At least I got paid, right?"

"Yes, Frank, that's right, at least you got paid," Mae said adding freshly picked herbs, spices, and red wine into the pot of tomato sauce. "Do you remember that lady on Westmoore Way, Frank? Lou, you probably don't remember because you were knee high, but I took you with me to personally ask this woman to please pay her past due bill. I had sent several reminders and she never replied to any of them. I don't know why your father didn't get paid before he left her house, but anyway, I held your little hand and knocked on this woman's door. She answered and I told her, respectfully, that we could really use the money; if she would please pay my husband for his work. I thought she would see that we were a family with bills like hers, maybe. Oh! The nerve of that woman! She told me she didn't have any money and to stop bothering her and she slammed the door in our faces! I just stood there shocked. You were so cute Lou. I'll never forget, you Lou. You looked up so cute and said, 'Don't worry Mommy, we'll go home and play until you feel better.' Anyway, I still don't believe that woman. I guess I was naïve. I know I wouldn't hire a man if I had no money to pay him." She took a spoon, dipped it in the pot and tasted her sauce. She went to the cupboard to put away the olive oil and get the flour and cocoa.

"By the way, I called that woman, Frances Doyle, Jim Doyle's sister."

"Yeah, here's another example, Lou. She says she the sister of a friend so I go right over and put a pump in her washer but then she doesn't pay me. I even gave her a discount."

"Well, when I called she said she had just put the check in the mailbox for that pump. I don't know why you didn't get paid before you left that job. Oh, no! I forgot about our oven." Mae felt the oven door with her hand. "Cold. I wanted to bake a cake for Julia and her father. It's so sad about their loss. Julia's mother was in my Garden Club and she was always very kind to everyone. You know Julia, don't you Lou?" She did not notice Lou blush but Frank did. He winked at him.

"Anyway," Mae continued, "I forgot our oven is broken."

"What? The oven's broken?" Frank and Lou said in tandem. They both sprung up and Mae had to step back or be run over. They felt the oven, checked the controls and without being asked, Lou took the keys Frank offered and went to the truck to get the toolbox.

"How long has it not been heating?" Frank asked.

"A couple of days, Doc," Mae said. Lou came in with the tool box and Frank asked for the volt/amp meter which Mae called 'the claw' because it looked like a giant one. Frank diagnosed the problem and gave Mae the prognosis.

"We're getting a new oven, Mae, how does that sound?"

"This is the best day I've had in a long time," she said stirring her marina with a long wooden spoon. "But tomorrow's gonna be better."

Twelve

WHEN EVELYN MET CHARLES

EVELYN had underestimated the length of Ricky's tentacles. She was shaken he had found her, but she renewed her determination to break from him.

Money was the first necessity. She got the job at 'The Coffee Shop.' The boss (a pot bellied, middle aged man who smelled like beer) took one look at her slender and curvaceous figure and scheduled her for nightly shifts.

On her first evening, she wore the employer supplied waitress uniform which was basically a bikini. Evelyn was thankful she had saved a pair of heels from her old job because each waitress was expected to provide her own shoes. The uniform was fine with her, she considered her body useful. And, the fact that management encouraged the waitress to reveal even more when particularly good customers were patronizing the bar, meant extra tips to make up for what Ricky stole.

After her first shift, she went to the bathroom to change into street clothes. She pulled on her old jeans, sweatshirt and jean jacket. She stuffed her little uniform in her backpack, and opened the ladies room door to leave. Leaning against the opposite wall was a tall, lithe man dressed in a collared, plaid shirt and expensive jeans.

"The Men's Room is down the hall," Evelyn said.

"That's a funny way to introduce yourself," he said smiling. "I'm Charles; it's nice to meet you finally." Evelyn recognized Charles from the bar but she was surprised he had noticed her. He was so good looking she could not hold the gaze of his penetrating hazel eyes.

"Sorry, I... my name is Evelyn."

Charles asked her to join him and they sat together at a table by the bar. They began comparing life stories and discovered they had a lot in common. They were both poor from a young age, and both had begun stealing in their youth. At age six, she stole candy and toys, then as she got older, food from grocery stores and clothing from department stores. She had never used a gun.

At first, he too stole from candy and toy stores, then from kids at school, then from random strangers. Growing taller and stronger, he and his friends would stalk weak, slow, or distracted people like jackals in the hunt for prey. He sometimes used a gun.

They both had been clean of drugs for awhile, and each expressed the desire to quit stealing and make their own way. Neither shared their most recent occupations.

They left the 'Coffee Shop' together and strolled down Main Street. Evelyn liked the feel of Charles' arm around her shoulder. She felt proud to walk in the company of such a handsome, affectionate man. She felt safe and protected by him, a feeling she remembered having with Ricky in better times.

"Hey, look in here," Charles said. They stopped at the windows of Dar's Jewelry Shop.

"I hate looking in there. It's just full of things I'll never have." She looked away.

"Baby, if I have anything to say about it, you'll have all this and more."

Thirteen

BE A MAN

FRANK woke to sunlight streaming through his bedroom window. He rolled over and draped his arm around Mae. Before Mae had gone in for her hospital stay, he had taken this pleasant contact for granted. The loneliness he had felt while she was in the hospital had passed with the summer heat. It was autumn but he still felt sheer gratitude for her presence.

He listened to her breath blow softly while she dreamed. He followed the lines on her face like trails over a beloved meadow. He did not see her age; he saw the same face he had loved at first sight.

When the grogginess of sleep lifted, Frank remembered it was Monday. He had made two important appointments that morning to which he must be on time. He threw off the warm blankets and rolled out of bed. He switched off the alarm he had not needed to wake him; and which Mae never needed. After his shower, he dressed in the shirt and pants Mae had ironed for him yesterday. She was still asleep when Frank left their room for the kitchen.

His search through the refrigerator revealed the sack lunch Mae had fixed last night. He reviewed the contents. A thermos of soup, a hunk of thickly buttered sourdough, and a bag of carrots. Not bad. The full carafe of coffee was the only evidence Lou was already awake. Frank helped himself to a hot travel cup of coffee, and before he left the house, wondered why Mae was still sleeping.

Frank always backed into his driveway. He liked his truck ready to go to work. He locked his sack lunch in a cargo box and opened the driver seat door.

"Hi Pop," Lou said. Frank wondered how, no matter how early he got going, Lou could beat him to the truck. He had been waiting for his father and now intended to join him on his service calls.

"Good Morning, Lou. I thought maybe you'd stay home today and get things ready before you start school again."

Lou thought his Dad was joking so he laughed. Frank was serious, but he was also late. He did not have time to argue, so he acquiesced to the stowaway.

Frank reconsidered his reluctance on the ride down the hill. It would be good to have Lou along for the two high profile calls that morning.

"OK, but listen up. This first repair could be trouble. The lady is a widow with money to burn. I hear through the grapevine she never uses a repairman twice because none of them are good enough for her. I'll handle the repair, I don't want any help." Frank looked over at Lou who smiled and nodded.

"The second repair is going to be fun. You've heard of Walt Whitman, right?" Frank asked.

Lou noticed a giddy tone in his Dad's voice. "Sure, he's caught for three Super Bowl championships hasn't he?"

"That's right son! And guess who he wants to fix his refrigerator? Huh? Me, that's who!"

Lou enjoyed seeing his father so animated for a change. Frank realized he was letting his excitement show. So, he toned it down with some fatherly advice.

"Lou, whatever line of work you land in…" (Lou rolled his eyes, and Frank continued,) "…you need a backbone and by that I mean you need to stand up for what you think is right. Now, in the repair business, it is a fact that most people are good, but there are people who will want something for nothing. For this reason, until I know which kind of person I am dealing with, I always insist my new customers pay me up front."

"Yeah, Mom always says we should get paid up front. It's not always easy though is it?" Lou asked diplomatically. He was aware Frances Doyle, a new customer, still had not paid his Dad for the pump he installed for her.

"No, it's not easy, it's right, Lou. Both customers are new today, so we will insist on being paid for our time." Frank knew such wealthy clients would insist on paying but at least Lou would see the policy in action. Changing the subject he asked, "School starts soon doesn't it?"

Frank may have changed the subject but the last subject had left a mark. What did he mean 'whatever line of work he landed in…'? What would it take for his Dad to officially partner with him? Did he think his son was not good enough at repair?

School did start soon, it was true, and Lou needed to tell his father it was starting without him. It was time to do the right thing.

"I guess it does start soon, yes Dad. But I'm not going back."

Frank said nothing, he was stunned. Somehow he knew, this was it. This was the mysterious tipping point when a parent must let go and give up control of their offspring's life. A moment before, Frank believed his son would complete the plans Frank and Mae had made for him. In this new moment, Lou declared his independence. He had made the same declaration to his own father.

"You're not going back," was the only response Frank could muster before talking to Mae. Lou remained silent.

The vistas on the way to the estate of Mrs. Davenport were breathtaking. Frank broke the silence with a bit of history.

"I wonder if San Francisco will want to cut all these redwoods down again. First, they used the redwoods to build new homes in San Francisco. Then the City came back for more after the 1906 earthquake and fire. Let's hope the third growth gets to stay."

They pulled into the estate and followed a redwood lined drive. The trees cleared to reveal a single spout fountain before a colossal, colonial mansion. The stables to the left of it and a smaller home to the right were smaller but built to match the main house. They drove around the circular driveway to a row of garage doors at the side of the mansion.

"Why don't you sit this one out," Frank said before getting out of the truck, but Lou had already gotten out of earshot, was out of the truck, and waiting at the side entrance of the home. Frank met his son at the door and rang the doorbell, twice, because no one answered the first time. Finally, a maid dressed in a traditional white uniform opened the door.

"The senora will not allow anyone in the house before 10:00 AM, please come back then, thank you." Without another word, she closed the door. Frank and Lou stared at the closed door, and then looked at each other.

"Mrs. Davenport called me and told me to be here first thing in the morning, and now she won't let me in the door? It's a good thing we have another call out here so we didn't waste the drive."

"Can I drive?" Lou asked. Frank's insides twisted.

"Sure, kid, but I feel a little pressure to get to these places on time. Let's finish the jobs first, and then you can drive home, OK?"

Lou agreed and before leaving the property, Frank took a little detour passed the guest cottage. It looked like a miniature of the main house but it was bigger than Frank's. The flower beds that graced the gabled windows reminded him of Mae's garden.

"You know, Lou, this place is impressive, but I wouldn't trade our home for it. We own it, and the land it sits on, free and clear. We have our own redwood tree and your Mom is an excellent gardener. So, we don't have a guest cottage? Guests are always welcome in our home."

This expression of appreciation startled Lou. In fact, his Dad had been uncharacteristically expressive all morning. Lou wondered if this new intimacy signified the start of a new relationship. Maybe his Dad finally was seeing him for the man he is. Lou straightened his back and pulled back his shoulders.

Frank found his way back to the main road and drove east. He drove a little faster the closer he got to the home of the esteemed football player's home. They found the address and pulled into another long driveway. Mrs. Davenport's property had been larger, but the Whitman home was as impressive. Two large chimneys flanked its giant sloping roof and a windowed turret jutted above the roof over the main entrance. A low, red sports car, and an SUV coated in ominous matte black were parked in the driveway which circled in front of the large arched entryway.

"You ready for this?" Lou asked.

"You bet I am," Frank answered.

They parked to the side of the property and took their toolboxes out of the truck. Frank smiled at the sight of Lou's box. Mae had given it to him for Christmas one year and Frank had given gifts of new tools every birthday and holiday.

A young woman let them in the house and led them through a long, arched hallway. They walked by a large dining room, a large sitting room, and many closed doors. They craned their necks down intersecting halls but did not catch a glimpse of the great Walt Whitman.

When they finally reached the cavernous kitchen, they began to work on the refrigerator. First, Lou helped Frank get the built-in refrigerator out of its cabinet space. They worked around each other, anticipating each other's next move like toreadors around a bull.

Unfortunately, not even the two working together could repair the football player's refrigerator. They cleaned up and pushed the refrigerator back into place.

"Hello, gentlemen," a silky baritone suddenly intoned from behind Frank and Lou. They turned around like shampoo commercial models who swing their long hair in slow motion. Walt Whitman had entered the kitchen and stood towering in their midst. Michelangelo's David would not have impressed Frank more. Mr. Whitman's eyes were piercing; the clothes he wore were fine and well fitting. Frank's eyes rapturously roamed the sports icon's figure until they met the chunky ring adorning Mr. Whitman's right hand. Lou elbowed his Dad.

"Mr. Whitman, it's so good to meet you. We are very big fans. Well, we're not, what am I saying, you're big, we're just fans… Anyway, we are *so* fans…" Frank stammered.

"Hi Mr. Whitman, I'm Lou, this is my dad, Frank. It's an honor to meet you." Lou and Frank reached out their hands and Walt Whitman shook them in turn.

"It's nice to meet you both, too. Please, call me Walt. I was just about to head out for a tee time but I wanted to check in to see how things were going with the refrigerator."

Remembering why he was in Walt Whitman's kitchen Frank said, "Well, I hate to say this but I have bad news, Walt. The compressor is the most expensive part on a refrigerator and yours has gone out. It's not worth it to replace because a new refrigerator doesn't cost much more than the repair would. We have the latest model of this refrigerator in stock. We can haul this one away and replace it today if you'd like," Frank offered.

"Sounds good, full service, I like that. Just send the bill to these guys." Walt handed Frank a card with the address of his football team's Management Office. Frank's heart sank. The words with which he had just lectured his son were still fresh in his mind, 'Do not leave a new customer until you get your money.' Then worse, fateful words echoed, 'No, doing the right thing is not easy, Lou, it's right.'

Why, Frank wondered, did Super Bowl Champ Walt Whitman have to witness a test of his character in front of his son? Why had he chosen that day to lecture Lou? Why did Walt Whitman have to be so tall? Lou looked at his Dad expectantly.

"Walt, again, I hate to say this but, my shop has a policy that I need to get paid before leaving the job. It would take an authorization from your team before I would get paid. So, I'm afraid I need to write a bill out to you personally."

Walt looked displeased. "Call me Mr. Whitman. How much for the repair?"

Frank answered him and Mr. Whitman retrieved a checkbook and wrote out a check. The large house was blanketed in silence. Handing the check to Frank he said, "Anyone too good to sell a refrigerator to my organization is too good to work for me anymore. Anita! Show these gentlemen out of my home, please." He left the kitchen, Lou and Frank's apologies hanging in the air behind him. Obediently, they followed Anita out of the kitchen and out of the front door.

"Well, Dad, you did the right thing..." Lou said.

"It doesn't feel like it," Frank admitted.

"Hey, it's not every day we get to meet a Super Bowl Champ." Lou slapped his Dad on the back.

Frank smiled and looked at his watch. "It's after ten o'clock. Maybe Mrs. Davenport will be kind enough to see us now."

Fourteen

CAN'T GET GOOD HELP

NEITHER THE SENORA nor the Maid answered the side entrance doorbell. Frank stepped back and looked up at the expansive side of the home. Out of the corner of his eye, he saw a sheer curtain fall into place in one of the far windows.

While Frank waited at the side door, Lou waited in the truck where he had a clear view of the stables. Gabled windows in the stable loft overlooked three paddocks laid out in front of the building like three picket framed yards. Every minute or so, a chestnut mare would come out of her home to check on Lou, and then disappear. He smiled at her coy glances. Suddenly, young man wearing western boots, cowboy hat, and bow legged, Lee jeans came out from behind the stable.

"Hi there! We're here to fix the dishwasher, do you know if anyone is home?" Lou called from the truck.

"Sorry, the maid left, but I can let you in," he said affably. The cowboy walked with Lou to the mansion and met Frank at the door. It irritated Frank that the maid had not mentioned her plan to leave.

The cowboy opened the door revealing a bright, wide, and long hallway. They followed him down the

84

hall passed pictures of barrel dodging horses and acrobatic women on horseback.

The first room they came to was a pantry the size of Frank's dinette at home. The room was lined with drawers and glass cabinets full of china, glassware, and every conceivable serving implement. A miniature glass chandelier lit the small room. In the back stood a luminous, floor to ceiling wine refrigerator. Stacked shelves full of corked bottles were visible behind a clear glass door.

"Check out that wine cooler. I'd like to get a look at the insides of that," Lou whispered. He was not a wine drinker, but both he and his Dad were intrigued by the gauges and mechanics of the specialized appliance. Frank made a mental note to stock some of these in his showroom.

"There's a dishwasher in here, and there's also one in the kitchen" the groom directed. "Oh, and the guest cottage has one too," he added.

"Well, which one is broken?" Frank asked.

"I don't know, I thought you knew," the groom answered. Frank's annoyance was growing.

"I know it's not your fault but your boss called me yesterday and told me to come out here by 9:00 this morning. Evidently, she gave me an inconvenient time, and now I don't know which dishwasher is broken. I have to go to each dishwasher and figure out if it's broken by trial and error. This lady has more money than brains," Frank vented.

"Don't worry, Dad, we'll figure this out. You take the kitchen and…" Before Lou diffused the situation, Mrs. Davenport appeared in the kitchen doorway.

"Excuse me. I couldn't help overhear your conversation with my stable hand. You may go, Enrico." Enrico blanched and was happy to exit the tension filled room.

"Sir, what was it you said about my brains and my money?" Mrs. Davenport stood in the kitchen doorway wearing white pants and a pink sweater. Her blond curls were draped behind ears adorned with dangling, pink earrings.

"M'am, have you been standing there listening to our conversation the whole time?" Frank asked.

"Yes, in fact I have," Mrs. Davenport said, a note of accusation in her tone.

"If you heard the conversation, why didn't you come out and tell us which dishwasher needed to be fixed?" Frank asked.

"I don't deal with hired men," she said. "I don't mean to be rude, I'm just being frank."

"Well, frankly, you won't have to deal with us anymore, M'am. Have a good day." He turned and strode down the hallway and out the door. Lou smiled kindly at Mrs. Davenport, and then followed his Dad toward the door.

"What about my dishwasher?" she called regally. Lou turned, smiled again, and quietly closed the door behind him.

"I'm driving, right?" Lou asked before his Dad could get to the driver side.

"Sure, kid. Take us back to the stables."

⧗

"You said what?" Mae stopped the office filing to face her husband.

"Look, I know I wasn't very polite, and I feel bad about that, but my time is important, Mae. If people jerk me around, that's time I'm not getting paid. We made two trips for that woman and we spent a lot of time waiting for someone to show up. Besides, when that lady overheard me asking her horse guy which dishwasher was broken, why didn't she come out and tell us which dishwasher to fix? She would never have come out if I didn't step on her fat ego."

"OK, OK, big guy. I don't want to spoil your good mood but I have more bad news," Mae said.

"When it rains it pours," Frank said.

"I called Jim's sister, Frances. She doesn't know why we didn't get a check for the washer pump but she doesn't think it's fair she should have to send another check."

"Not fair? But it's fair that she doesn't pay for her new pump and my labor?"

"OK, look, I'll keep working on her, don't worry about it," Mae said.

"No, Mae, that's it, I've had it. I'm taking matters into my own hands. Oh, by the way, which oven do you want? Exelda's coming by later to pick up our old one so if you don't decide today, you won't have an oven tonight."

"Well, twist my arm why don't you? I'll take a Thermador." Mae said.

"Your wish is my command."

"Oh? Then I command you not to confront Frances Doyle over her pump bill. I don't want things to get heated."

"Mae, trust me," Frank said reassuringly.

Fifteen

TAKE THE CAKE

"LOU, what's gotten into you? You always deliver my cakes!"

"Mom, it's different this time. It's late. And, Julia… Julia… Forget it, I'll take it." He picked up the covered cake plate from the counter and left the kitchen before Mae could ask any more questions. Frank surprised them both by coming through the front door.

"Hey, where's the fire?" Frank asked. Lou passed him quickly and pulled the front door shut behind him. Frank glanced at the door and joined Mae in the kitchen.

"It is freezing out there! Just starting to rain." Frank shook his coat out and hung it on a kitchen chair. "What's up with Lou, Mae? His face was the color of your marinara sauce."

Mae filled her mixing bowl with soapy water and began swirling the sides of the bowl with her sponge. "I'm not sure but I think he might have a crush on Julia McCauley. I baked a cake for her and her father, I feel so sad for them. Poor girl, losing her mother so young. Usually, Lou loves delivering my cakes, but when I asked him this time, he got flustered. It's so cute. Anyway, where have you been? You didn't say where you were going. What's that?" she asked pointing a wet finger to a washer pump in his hand.

"It's a washer pump."

"Actually, I did know that. What I mean is, where did it come from?"

"Well, Mae, it's like this. You know the pump I installed in Frances Doyle's washer? Well, I figured, she didn't pay for it. What's more, she's not going to pay for it. So, I took it back."

"Frank! Are you serious? Wait, what do you mean exactly? How did you take it back from her?"

"It wasn't that difficult actually. I went to her house hoping to reason with her, but she wasn't home. Her son was home and he let me in. I simply went to the washer, removed the pump, and left the house. Boom, end of story."

"That's a relief. You know, that could have been nasty, Frank. I'm glad it worked out. Now, on to the next pressing issue…. which is… my new oven almost burned my cake for the McAuleys."

"Mae, different ovens cook differently, you have to adjust the temperature sometimes."

"Oh, so it's a case of 'the cook not the oven'? I know that happens but would you mind checking it, Frank? This cake recipe has been in my family for generations of ovens and we've all used the same oven temperature."

Frank got the temperature tester and clamped it on the rack. With a quick diagnosis, he determined the setting for the oven temperatures were accurate.

"Mae, it's working fine, sometimes it's not the oven you know, it's the cook."

"Well, I'm not sure I like this oven, Frank. It's not like my old one, or my mother's old one, or…"

"Mae! I got the best oven money could buy for you and you don't like it? It even cleans itself! Oh."

"What do you mean, 'Oh'?" Mae asked hopefully. Frank blushed slightly.

"Oh… wait a minute. There's something you should know about self cleaning ovens, Mae."

"What's that, Frank?"

"They have a little more insulation in them, so they stay off longer once it reaches the temperature you set."

"Oh! Now you tell me. I'm going to have to play with the temperature next time. No one in my family has ever had a self cleaning oven. I guess I can keep the new oven after all." She went back to the sink. "I tell you, baking that cake has me pooped. I'm going to go to bed early, you coming?" She finished washing up and turned out the kitchen light.

It never ceased to amaze Frank how problems between him and Mae passed like shooting stars. One minute they were arguing about the new oven, the next minute they were going to bed together.

The phone woke them both. It was seven thirty on Saturday morning, and they had intended to sleep in.

"Hello?" Mae answered groggily.

"Mae, look out your window!"

"Dar? Is that you?"

"Yes! Mae, it is me Dar, look out your window!"

"What does he want?" Frank asked.

"He wants us to look out the window. OK, OK, Dar, don't worry we'll get up and look out the window.

Thanks for calling, OK?" Mae hung up the phone, pulled the covers over her shoulders and snuggled into her pillow. Frank was now wide awake and looked at Mae incredulously.

"Mae, what are you doing? Come on, get up, maybe he was serious. Unless he was drinking, but that's not like Dar." He bumped her shoulder gently. Finally Mae roused and they both got out of bed.

Frank pulled back the curtain to reveal a dazzling sight. Though autumn had barely arrived, the yard, trees, and plants were blanketed in a soft layer of white snow. Ice crystals bejeweled Mae's tomato plants making them sparkle brilliantly. The world had changed overnight.

"Well, what do you know? Do you ever remember getting snow this time of year?" Mae asked.

"Mom! Dad!" Lou called from the yard. He had run outside and was scooping up snow with his bare hands. He grinned mischievously and hurled a little snowball at their window. Mae and Frank dressed quickly and went outside to return the assault. Frank threw a nice sized snowball at Lou, but Lou ducked and the missile flew harmlessly into the street. Just then, a police car pulled up and rolled over the snow splash.

Frank recognized his old friend, Jim Geraghty in the driver seat. They had played football in school together. Jim got out of his patrol car and walked over to the shivering family. Mae was not used to seeing her husband's old buddy in uniform. He swaggered like John Wayne in an old western, his arms held out from his sides to clear all of the gear on his belt.

"Hey Jim, how are you? What do you think about all this snow?" Frank asked.

"Yeah, this weather is really something. Good morning Mae, Lou. Frank, I hate to do this, but I'm here on official business. I have a warrant for your arrest."

Mae laughed but Frank saw the look in his friend's eyes. Jim was wearing a sympathetic but determined expression and Frank understood his friend meant business.

"Why, Jim, what for?" Frank asked.

"A citizen by the name of Frances Doyle has reported you for stealing a pump out of her washer. Do you know anything about that?"

"She what? You know who that is, Jim? That's Jim Doyle's sister. We went to school with him. I did her a favor by rushing over to her place and putting a damn pump in her washer. She refused to pay for it! Mae even worked on her. So I took it back. It's my pump until she pays for it." Frank's breath steamed in the cool morning air.

"OK, Frank, let some air out of your tires, OK? Look, I'm not a judge, but I do know that once you put a part in someone else's machine, it belongs to them. If you have a problem getting paid then you have to go to court about it. Now, the way I see it, you have two options. I can take you to jail, and you can tell it to the judge. Or, you can put the pump back in Frances Doyle's washer. What do you say?"

Mae had gone white. Lou was amazed. He had thought the early snow was a phenomenon but his Dad's warrant trumped the weather.

"Fine. I'll put it back. The pump is in the house. I'll go get it and be right out," Frank conceded. He brought the family into the house, each of their hearts threatening to pound through their chests.

The pump was in Frank's storage locker. He had stored it next to the white jewelry box he had gotten at Dar's. He was glad he had waited to give Mae the diamond ring it contained. If he got into any more trouble with Frances Doyle, it would give Mae a lift.

Sixteen

OUT OF ORDER

FRANCES and Officer Geraghty exchanged pleasantries while Frank put the pump back into Frances' washer. In the middle of the installation, Frank's little cell phone rang. It was Linda Straisburg calling. He paused the installation while he took the call.

"Sure, Linda but I'm telling you there's nothing wrong with your refrigerator. If I make it any colder you'll have to eat your ice cream with an ice pick... OK, OK. I'll be over in half an hour."

Frank finished the pump job and Officer Geraghty, satisfied with the installation, asked the involved parties to sign off on his paperwork.

"Frank, thank you so much for installing my pump. Again. Don't worry about the check I mailed. I'm sure your wife will find it when she gets organized," Frances said. She escorted the men out of her home.

"Call me if you have any more problems," Frank said. Officer Geraghty raised his eyebrows but refrained from comment until they got back to the patrol car.

"Were you offering to work on her washer again?" Officer Jim asked.

"Off the record?" Frank asked.

95

"Off the record, just don't tell me you did anything illegal."

"Look, you said I had to put the pump back. You didn't say I had to connect it," Frank said. He looked at Jim.

Jim laughed and started the car. "I think the law is definitely on your side this time, Frank." He dropped Frank off at his service truck and they promised to meet for a beer soon.

Frank was happy to leave his legal troubles behind, but wondered what troubles lay before him with Linda Straisburg and her freezer. He took his time driving up the freeway, parked in front of her apartments, trudged out of his truck and stepped cautiously on the path to her office.

"Hey Linda, how are you?"

"Well, I am well. And you, how are you, Frank?"

"I'm fine Linda. How is your husband, is he still in the hospital?"

"Oh, no, he's out. Actually, he's dead. I mean, he died in the hospital and now he's out. It was all very sudden … and sad," she added.

"Well, I am truly, very sorry to hear that, Linda. My sympathies."

"Thank you, dear Frank. I can always count on your strong shoulders to lean on."

"And, Mrs. Peyton? Is she doing any… better?" Frank asked, eager to change the subject.

"Mrs. Peyton is recovering from her loss, thank you for your concern. Now, I do have the matter of my freezer. Will you follow me to my apartment?"

Linda Straisburg's apartment was on the ground floor and it was the first time Frank had been inside it.

He expected to find a formal, traditional living style to match Linda's formal demeanor but what he saw surprised him. The wooden floor of the living room had been painted white, and a white bear rug lay in front of a white washed fireplace. An oversized, black sketch of a nude woman biting a red apple hung above the mantle. Frank's eyes rested on the drawing before noticing the white couch, white walls and deep red, oversized leather chair in the corner.

"Please follow me to the kitchen," Linda invited warmly.

Frank followed her into the kitchen which, like the living room, was decorated in white, except for the stainless steel appliances. She opened the door to her freezer.

"Now, reach in here and tell me what you feel. I don't think it's cold enough but I'm afraid to put the setting any lower. I don't like hard ice cream," she said. She took a piece of ice from the ice bin and put it in her mouth.

Several of the buttons on Linda's white blouse, normally covered by a neck scarf, were undone. Frank noticed because it was the first time he remembered seeing Linda without a scarf. Even more curious was that she had a piece of ice in her mouth when she did not like hard ice cream. He decided to focus on the freezer temperature.

As Frank reached into the freezer, Linda leaned close to him. His hand cooled the instant he felt her warm breath on his cheek. At the sound of the ice cube rolling over in her mouth Frank turned to her, and noticed the color of her tongue was a shade pinker than the glossy lipstick she had slathered on her lips.

Frank refocused on the freezer. Clearly, there was nothing wrong if the ice cubes were perfectly formed. To humor her, he could monitor the temperature with a twenty four hour temperature chart. If he used the chart, he'd have to return the next day to read it. It was disconcerting to think of returning the next day with Linda behaving so strangely. He had heard of lonely women who made up phony appliance problems in exchange for the company of a repairman. Frank might notice an attractive woman, but his devotion to Mae never strayed.

At last, a solution came to him. He lowered the temperature dial. Linda would observe the cooler setting. However, to keep the ice cream from getting too hard, he quickly adjusted the internal setting on the control. Technically, the temperature of the freezer would stay the same, but he hoped the adjustment would cool Linda off.

"OK, I think we're good now, Linda. I lowered the setting but you'll still be able to get a spoon into your ice cream." He picked up his toolbox and walked quickly toward the front door. His sudden exit startled Linda, and she accidentally swallowed her ice cube.

"What? Are you done already? I was just… well, then… I certainly appreciate your visit. I'll look forward to seeing you next time, Frank. Please, stop by any time," she said sweetly.

"Thanks Linda, I'll let myself out." Frank shut the door behind him and he did not slow down until he was out of the building. On the way to the truck, Frank's cell phone rang.

"Yeah Lou, what is it?"

"It's Mom, you need to come home, now."

98

Seventeen

THE FUNERAL

MAE had just come home from her garden club meeting. She was too tired to stay and chat afterward with the ladies, but she was excited about the sunflower seeds she got in a trade for her heirloom tomato seeds. It was too late in the year to plant them so she would keep them in the dark garden shed. She closed the seed box and marveled how life could spring from such a dark place. Though the temperature was cool, she wiped perspiration from her forehead. Needing to sit, she closed up the shed and went into the house.

Thanksgiving was near, so after she changed into her slippers, she found her big box of recipe cards and sat at the kitchen table. She searched for the most decadent desserts and rich side dishes she had ever made. She had hoped sitting would relieve her fatigue, but she began to feel worse.

The pain she called indigestion was pulling on her chest. She had promised her doctor she would call him if she had symptoms like this, but the timing was bad. The holidays were coming and she could not be sick.

She reached for a stuffing recipe card but haltered. She caught her breath in wonder. Never had she felt a stab of pain so strong! It was coming from between her shoulder blades so she leaned back on the chair to put pressure on it.

Random thoughts wove through the pain. Perhaps this was how a knife stab felt. Frank would worry if she got sick again. He shouldn't worry. Frank. How she loved him. Lou. Sweet Lou.

The thought of leaving them alone filled her chest with sorrow and guilt. She stood and went to the phone, but her arms felt like dead wood limbs.

She would sit a moment until her energy returned. She crouched to the floor, her knee resting on the cool tile. It felt good in this position and she began to feel better. She decided she would give herself a break from making dinner and defrost a casserole from the freezer.

She put her hand on the floor for leverage to stand. Suddenly, the pain intensified, wrapped around her chest, grabbed hold of her heart, squeezed, and stabbed her through. She surrendered and shrank to the floor, leaning against the telephone table. Tears fell heavy down her cheeks. She wanted desperately to say good bye to her family. Frank. Sweet Lou... How she loved...

Mae suffered a fatal heart attack. Lou found her sitting in a slouched position on the floor, near the phone in the hallway. Perhaps, he thought, she had wanted to call for help. He lifted her chin. Despite her open eyes, he wanted to believe his mom, his best friend, was still alive.

He reached over her for the phone. First, Lou called 911, then his Dad, and finally he called the church. The church secretary, usually busy and overwhelmed, was kind. She promised to send Fr. Gio to the house right away. With no other calls to make, Lou sat in the living room from where he could stare at his mother's slippered foot. He felt numb except for a dark ache in his heart.

Frank arrived and crumpled to his knees when he saw Mae. He rocked her lifeless body and sobbed until the coroner arrived with a police officer. The officer apologized for the few questions she must ask. She had served on the police force long enough, however, to know these men had nothing to do with Mae's death.

"Father Gio, come in." Frank welcomed their pastor into the house, steering him passed the coroner who was preparing to take Mae's body. Fr. Gio and Frank had never been close but on this day, they were brothers in grief.

Gio loved Mae who often invited him to dinner with her family. Frank would ignore the priest for a ballgame on TV, but Lou would join Mae and Fr. Gio's lively conversations. Fr. Gio's memories of Mae flowed freely with his tears. Finally, he pulled himself together and put one hand on each of the men's shoulders.

"You men are not alone. Everyone loved Mae and if anything, I think you should be prepared for a barrage of love and support from your community. It's just so sudden, I can't believe it." Fr. Gio's voice cracked and Lou put his arm around him. The three men watched Mae's covered, lifeless form taken out of the house, passed her garden, and into the little, white coroner's van.

⧗

When Mae heard of a sad or happy event in her small town, she wanted to share in it. Over the years, there were many families who had been touched by her kindness. Mae had baked cakes for wakes and knitted blankets for countless new babies.

Now it was the community's turn to share the family's sorrow and it packed the church for Mae's funeral. Of course, Mae's friends from the garden club were there. Linda Straisburg, in a dark red suit, white scarf, and large sunglasses, sat in the third row on the aisle. Her hair was pulled into a tight bun on the back of her head and she dabbed her eyes with a small white handkerchief. Dar the jeweler dotted his eyes with tissue and sat alone behind Linda Straisburg. He stared trancelike at her hair bun. Lamar and Exelda, Frank's business partners attended the funeral with hearts full of grief for the loss of a friend, and in sympathy for Frank and Lou. Many of Frank's customers dotted the congregation including the Bicho brothers, who arrived late and left early.

Frank and Lou were grateful for everyone's presence but they remained in shock over losing Mae. They processed down the aisle with the casket and stood side by side in the first pew, feeling the warmth of each other's shoulder.

The service began. Fr. Gio's voice intoned somberly. Frank stared at the ceiling and remembered the moment thirty years before, under this same roof, when a priest pronounced him and Mae married.

Fr. Gio asked everyone to be seated. The service proceeded and Lou picked at a blister on his palm. He occasionally glanced at the casket in the aisle next to him thinking it strange it contained anyone, let alone his mother. He happened to look over the casket and discovered Julia in the opposite pew seated beside her father. She smiled sympathetically at him. Lou looked away quickly.

He remembered his recent, awkward cake delivery. Julia had opened her front door with a friendly smile and greeting. Lou had practically shoved the cake at her, mumbled sympathy over her mother's death, and turned to leave like a jack rabbit in fear for its life. Seeing Julia at his own mother's funeral, he pondered the obvious question. What was it about Julia that made him behave so strangely? Everyone who knew Lou liked Lou. He was easy going with everyone. It did not matter if they were pretty girls, old women, or big burly men, he remained his affable self. What was it about Julia that stopped his breathing and made him blush all over?

On the altar, Fr. Gio looked sad, which one might expect at a funeral, except that Fr. Gio did not look sad at every funeral. Sometimes he looked relieved, particularly if an irritating member of the flock had passed on. At the pulpit, Fr. Gio presented his carefully prepared reflection. He began slowly and became animated as the sermon continued. Just before his homily reached its crescendo, lifting up Mae as an example of service to one's neighbor, he lost the attention of the congregation.

A garbled, loud voice echoed through the church. It seemed to come and go which distracted the grieving congregants who looked around in confusion. Fr. Gio continued his homily, but between impassioned examples of Mae's selflessness, he scoured the church for the source of the disruption. Finally, long time family friend, Officer Geraghty, covertly found the volume on his police radio and silenced it.

Neighbors and friends stopped by the house after the funeral, offering words of encouragement to Lou and Frank. Linda Straisburg gave Frank a wink and a business card, "call me XO" written on the back of it. Casseroles filled their refrigerator. Cakes and cookies covered their dining room table.

The nights were the hardest for Frank and Lou. It was in the early hours of the dark day that they wondered what would become of themselves without Mae. Could life go on as it had without her?

Eighteen

THE CHAINS THAT BIND

"SERIOUSLY RICKY? I haven't even been here a week!" Evelyn held the door with her left foot to keep Ricky from coming inside.

"I'm so sorry I can't stay long. Just give me my share, honey, and I'll let you stay the month," Ricky threatened.

Evelyn looked into Ricky's soft brown eyes. She had loved him once. She would give him money this time, but it was the last time. Bracing the door, she stretched to the closet to reach her jacket.

"Here. That's all I have Ricky, you didn't give me enough time. But I'll have lots more soon. I like it here. I think this is going to work with us this time," she lied.

"It's going to work all right. Here, I have a present for you." He put a little cellophane packet of white powder in her hand. Evelyn looked at it as if it would burn a hole through her.

"I don't do this shit anymore, Ricky."

"Think of it as a lifeline. You know things get rough sometimes."

Nineteen

TV DINNER

FRANK AND LOU picked over their dinners. They had decided not to celebrate Thanksgiving but friends had delivered turkey and all the fixings so they were aware of the holiday. They sat together at the kitchen table watching a college game on TV. Mae would never have let them watch TV while they ate because she could not ignore the two men she loved most. Besides, she loved to share the day's stories with them. Lou had loved those dinners too but since his mother died, he had no interest in conversation. Frank had never had the interest so TV filled the silence.

Frank looked away from the game. He looked at Lou who had been so strong for him, graciously receiving the avalanche of community support, protecting his reticent father. But when he was not shielding his father, Lou was silent and inactive. Frank had to do something to help his son.

"Lou, I've been thinking about something." Frank put his fork down and paused the game. Lou left his eyes on the TV a moment, and then slowly looked down to his plate, almost surprised to see there was food in front of him.

"Sure, Dad, what's that?"

"Lou, I want you to partner with me," his father said. Lou looked up from his plate and regarded his father. Had he just heard what he thought he had heard? How many years had he waited for his father to say these very words?

Suddenly, his plans to lie on the couch, eat, and watch TV were waylaid. His father's request felt like a bolt of energy shot through his body. Frank was relieved (but a little nervous) to see the spark in his son's eyes again. His one regret was that Mae could not see her son's joy.

"I'll start Monday," Lou said more calmly than he felt.

"Monday, it is," Frank said more calmly than he felt.

Twenty

THE START OF SOMETHING WONDERFUL

THE WEEKEND could not pass quickly enough for Lou. He slept fitfully Sunday night and woke an hour before his alarm would have awakened him. He quickly showered, and dressed like his dad in a light green shirt and khaki pants. In the kitchen, he made the coffee, boiled some eggs, and started the toast. After ten long minutes, he ate two boiled eggs, a piece of buttered toast, a banana, a bowl of instant oatmeal and yogurt. When he was finished eating, he cleaned up, and sat expectantly at the kitchen table. Finally, his father walked into the kitchen, bleary eyed but showered and dressed.

"I see you're ready for work." Frank said.

"I wouldn't want to keep my boss waiting for me on my first day," Lou answered, his eyes twinkling with joy. Frank trudged over to the coffee pot, grabbed a mug, and filled it with the black brew. "I didn't sleep well last night. I kept waking up because I thought your mother was there." He took one of the eggs out of the pot and peeled it at the sink.

"Yeah, I didn't sleep very well either," Lou said, though the reason was anticipation. "Your bag lunch is on the counter. I made some sandwiches last night from the leftover turkey. There's a mug of soup and an apple too. Oh, and I threw in some cookies that the neighbors brought over," Lou said.

Frank marveled at the healthy appetite of his son. He finished his coffee. Silently, Frank took the heavy lunch bag and his keys from the counter and went out the front door. They got into the truck, and began their journey to the shop. Lou chattered all the way, while Frank shaded the sun from his eyes.

"OK, Dad! Let's do the ritual of the keys!" Frank's method of unlocking the shop had amused Lou since childhood. First, Frank pulled the keys from his retractable key ring and inserted the key to unbolt the lock. Always the bolt first, he had told his son for years. Next, he inserted the key to turn the knob, and pushed on the door with his left index finger while his right hand removed the key.

No matter how often he opened his shop in the morning, Frank relished the view after he pushed door open with his index finger. His eyes ran down the shiny floors of the hallway to the showroom where most of the new appliances were displayed. Because of the weather and sun position, the shop looked a little different every day. This time the bright morning sunlight was streaming through the giant showroom windows and bouncing off of the dazzling appliances.

Frank wanted to take the first week with Lou slowly. He wanted to judge Lou's patience level and add responsibility gradually.

"What's that?" Lou asked.

"It's a garbage disposal I got from the Straisburg apartment. I haven't had time to fix it. Why don't you make some coffee? Watch and learn this week, Lou. I want you to learn the business the right way. From the ground up."

For the first week of official employment, Lou spent most of his time sitting in the office, across from Frank's desk in the visitor's chair. It was comfortable but not what Lou had had in mind when his dad offered him a job. Besides making coffee, he answered the phone and took orders for service calls. The days churned slowly through the hours.

At 3:00 on Friday afternoon, Lou considered the garbage disposal in the "to be fixed" area. It had been there all week. Lou was restless, and full of pent up desire to fix something. It was possible, Lou thought, that his Dad wanted him to fix it. His father had left him in the same room with a broken gadget. Perhaps it was a test?

Lou stood up from his chair and crossed over to the workbench. He checked the doorway to see if he was alone, and then checked the motor with a meter. The start and run wiring was OK. He went back to his chair and sat down. He listened carefully for his father's footsteps but heard nothing. He stood up, went to the workbench, and checked the power cord which he determined was not frayed. He turned quickly, went back to his chair, and sat down again. His knee bounced rapidly while he considered his next move. Finally, he stood up, approached the bench, and stripped the wire where the cord to the motor switch was connected.

The sound of the working disposal beckoned his wide-eyed father to the office door. Lou was so excited at the life he had brought forth he had forgotten all about his Dad. Then, Frank cleared his throat.

110

Lou turned slowly to face his father who was staring at the grinding garbage disposal. Frank had not been able to fix it. Lou unplugged the disposal. The phone rang.

"Thought I was going to have to trash that. I'll get the phone, head out to the showroom," Frank said matter of factly.

Lou left the office with a sigh of relief. His eyes adjusted to the glare from the showroom windows in time to greet a customer entering the shop. Lou was excited to be out of the office and able to have face to face customer contact. He demonstrated his superior repair abilities, now he would show his Dad what he could do on the sales floor. Lou greeted the customer enthusiastically and began to work, what he liked to call, 'his magic.'

Meanwhile, Frank was taking service orders. He got two calls in a row about new appliances that could not clean. He finished the calls and realized he had left his novice employee unattended in the showroom. He quickly made his way out of the office.

As he entered the showroom, he overheard his son declare triumphantly to a departing customer, "Yes Sir, a lifetime warranty! Thank you *very* much. See you this afternoon."

Frank stopped short, raised his eyebrows, and waited for the customer to leave.

"Lifetime warranty, Son?"

"Sure!"

"Son, we don't offer lifetime warranties on anything in our showroom," Frank said, more calmly than he felt.

"But Dad, did you see how old that guy was?"

"I did."

"Well, one of our refrigerators will outlast him for sure!"

"Lou, you might be right but remember our policy, OK? We can't go around making false guarantees no matter how old the customers are."

"OK Dad, sorry."

"OK, now, what time did you promise the delivery?"

"By five o'clock."

Frank calculated the hours left in the day. There was barely enough time to get the two service calls done before the delivery. And, there was another problem. Should Frank send Lou on the repairs, or leave him at the shop?

"Lou, do you think you're ready to go on your first service call? It's fine if you're not, it's a big responsibility representing me … I mean representing the company."

"Dad, I can do this. I've watched you for years; I know I can handle it."

"OK, Lou. But, listen. You won't satisfy the first lady, Mrs. Faxon, because she's never satisfied. I've been to her house and already checked her washer. There is nothing wrong with it. Just be polite and humor her, but don't charge her. The second lady probably doesn't know how to use her appliance because it's new. Show her how it works but don't charge her either. And on the last call, Lou, just deliver the refrigerator and get out of there. Look at me. I never shoot the breeze with my customers. Keeps me out of trouble."

Twenty-One

PLANNING FOR THE FUTURE

EVELYN AND CHARLES sat together in her reclining chair. Charles lifted Evelyn's chin and assured her he had thought of everything.

"Baby, it's gonna be there and all we have to do is take it. The Indian will let us in, and he won't suspect a thing because you're so damn beautiful. Who wouldn't want to marry you? Once we got it, you take it and keep it safe." Charles brusquely kissed Evelyn for emphasis.

"But why? Why do we have to split up? Why can't we leave together?" Evelyn asked.

"You got to trust me, Evy. They'll be looking for two people together, so we have to separate. And I want you to keep the diamond because you're gonna be my wife. See? I trust you, baby." Charles knew if he was caught with the stolen diamond, he would be sent back to prison. He promised himself he would never go back there. He kissed her again, so hard this time it hurt her lips.

Twenty-Two

ALONE

FRANK watched from the back door of the shop. He put a hand on the small of his back while his son loaded and tied down the new, "guaranteed" refrigerator inside the truck. Lou jumped down from the truck and grabbed the rope to pull down the rolling cargo door. He waved to his Dad and jumped into the driver's seat. His heart beat with the excitement of his first solo service call. He had every confidence in himself, but he knew he had to earn the confidence of his Dad. He drove out of the parking lot slowly, so his Dad would not worry.

Unfortunately, driving slowly did not prevent Frank from worrying. What if Lou wrecked the truck? What if he wrecked the appliances? What if he insulted the customer, and word got out that his business was going downhill?

He went back into the shop and remembered that Mae liked to give Lou cakes and gifts to deliver because he was so friendly. Simultaneously, he was consoled and saddened by the memory of Mae.

Meanwhile, Lou drove the speed limit and played one of Frank's mantras "with trust comes responsibility" in his head. He was glad his Dad trusted him but he had the nagging feeling that nothing he did was good enough. What about the garbage disposal he repaired? His Dad's reaction was lukewarm. He said nothing about his first big sale except to criticize the lifetime guarantee Lou offered. Approval always seemed just beyond Lou's reach.

Lou took a bit out of a leftover cookie he found on the passenger seat. The jolt of sugar snapped him out of his pity party. Lou knew it was hard for his dad to be without his mom. He also knew he was no substitute for her companionship in the same way he knew his dad was no substitute for his mom.

He arrived at the Atherton address, parked out front, and strutted up the brick pathway toward a gracious home. Before ringing the bell, he realized his toolbox was still in the truck. He went back to the truck, retrieved it, and strutted again up the pathway to the vine-covered porch. The doorbell called a pooch to duty and soon the woman of the house opened the door.

"Oh, I'm so glad you're here," welcomed Mrs. Faxon. She was a short, pudgy woman with white skin and hair.

"When I spoke to your Father I explained that today is Friday, and I always do my wash on Friday, but what's the use if my washer isn't spinning?"

Lou reached down and pet the curious beagle who sniffed his toolbox. "Hey little pooch, you're a good guard dog aren't you?" The beagle sniffed again and trotted off to his bed by the door. He looked suspiciously at Lou.

"My grandmother never had a specific wash day, Mrs. Faxon, because she loved to hang her laundry outside on clothes lines. And you know, if it was nice on Friday, wash day was Friday."

Mrs. Faxon smiled and said, "Here's the washer right through here Lou. My mother used to hang our wash outside on lines too. I still see those big sheets blowing in the wind. My sister and I played tag between them."

Lou started the washer and they entertained each other with memories of spring wind until Mrs. Faxon's washer cycle spun to an end.

At the final buzzer, Mrs. Faxon looked at Lou. This was the moment of truth. She was sure her washer was broken but no one believed her. She reached into the washer, pulled out the clothes, and held them in the air like a trophy. "See! Not spun enough!" She declared. Lou felt the clothes and was not convinced. Mrs. Faxon seemed like a nice lady so he decided to help her out.

"Ah! I know what's wrong. Why didn't I think of this before?"

Mrs. Faxon watched hopefully while Lou pulled the front panel off the washer. He rummaged through his toolbox and found a tiny screwdriver and flashlight. He shone the flashlight toward the motor compartment and said aloud, "I thought so."
Leading with the screwdriver, he reached the length of his arm into the machine. He turned the screwdriver twice clockwise, shone the light again, and said, "There, now let's try it."

Lou ran another spin cycle and gave Mrs. Faxon a history lesson about classic wringer washers. He had developed a fascination with antique washers when he was a boy. Mae would take him on special outings to the library and together they would pore over all the antique machinery books they could find. When the spin cycle finished, Mrs. Faxon opened the door, pulled out the bundle, and declared the load properly spun.

"Well, aren't you a miracle worker, Lou?! I guess I won't be asking for your father next time. I knew I was right about my washer! You're an excellent repairman, Lou," said Mrs. Faxon, planting a grateful kiss on his cheek.

"Thanks Mrs. Faxon. No charge, we should have thought of that sooner," Lou said, realizing he did not know how much to charge anyway. He would have to ask his Dad about fees.

Before leaving, he pet the beagle, and he assured Mrs. Faxon of many happy cycles with her new washer. He did not, however, make a guarantee.

On his way to the next service call, Lou weighed the ethics of repair. Truthfully, there was nothing wrong with Mrs. Faxon's washer. On the one hand, his father had told the truth and left the customer unhappy. Lou, on the other hand, had tweaked the truth and left the customer happy. Lou pretended to tighten a loose screw. What was the harm in that? Mrs. Faxon felt vindicated and Lou left a hero. He shivered. His mother would have had an opinion. Would it have been, 'you helped the poor lady, Lou' or, 'the right thing is not easy, it's right, Lou'?

It was almost lunchtime so Lou ate one of his sandwiches while he drove toward Franklin Valley on Woodside Road. It was not as tasty as the ones his mother used to make.

Fearing too much traffic, he took Alameda down to Sandy Hill Road. He drove passed land, which in the 1800s, belonged to Mexico. The land had changed hands and now belonged to large estate and farm owners. Groves of towering redwood trees peppered the route.

Lou arrived at the Franklin Valley address and drove up a shady, long driveway to a cobblestoned courtyard. He remembered being at the house (which the old owners had called a Chateau) with his Dad but new owners lived there now. A raven-haired beauty came out of the house and met Lou at the truck. She wore cowboy boots, jeans, and a blue button down shirt. Mother of pearl buttons strained to keep the shirt closed.

Maria Gutierrez introduced herself and explained she and her husband Paul were new to the neighborhood. She was having trouble with the dishwasher they had purchased recently in New York before their cross-country move.

"That's a long way to move, how do you like it out here so far?" Lou asked.

"Oh, honey, I love it! Most of my family lives back east and I can't deny that's a bonus. My family is a handful, let me tell you! Really though, we decided to go west for the weather and we haven't been disappointed," Maria said.

"I love the weather around here. This is supposed to be winter but it's warmer than the rest of the country!" Lou said.

"This weather makes my husband happy too. He's retired but he's not finished working. He wants to make wine. He planted rows and rows of beautiful little grape vines in the backyard," she explained, leading Lou inside the house and into her cavernous kitchen.

"Next spring you'll have some picking to do! So, this is the dishwasher giving you trouble?" Lou asked walking toward the shiny, new appliance.

"Yes, it is, Lou honey. It is so sad that a new dishwasher cleans so poorly. I wanted to scrap it and buy another brand but my husband suggested I call a repairman first. My neighbors recommended your shop. They have been *so* helpful getting us acquainted with the area."

"Oh? Who are your neighbors?"

"The Plummers. They are just a lovely couple."

"Oh sure, they're a great couple. They have a black lab named Terry, don't they?"

"Yes, they do! Terry is just a lovely dog. Sometimes they take him out on trail rides with their horses. He's a bit heavy so the exercise does him good. I hope they ask me to ride with them some day! I just love horseback riding. I'm thinking of getting a horse myself."

"A vineyard and a horse? Good thing you're on a lot of land here, Maria! OK, let's load up the dishwasher and wash a quick cycle."

Maria smiled, showed Lou the dirty dishes already in the washer, and poured the detergent into the dishwasher.

"Uh, Maria ..."

"Yes, Lou honey?"

"That's the steam vent you're pouring the powder into."

"Are you sure, Lou? That's where I put the soap."

Lou took off the dishwasher door panel, and a shower of soap powder cascaded to the floor.

"Oh! Well, how did all that soap get in there? No wonder my dishes weren't clean!"

"Maria, the soap goes here, in the little door with the lid," Lou demonstrated.

"Oh, I see! Well, bless your heart, I guess my dishwasher isn't broken. We haven't hired a maid yet and I guess I have a lot to learn." She picked up an orange and started to peel it. "Do you want some orange, Lou?"

"No, thanks, Maria, I just ate. This is a very nice dishwasher, it should work just fine once we get it all cleaned up. But how long has your fridge been making that noise?" Lou had focused on the dishwasher and ignored the rackety refrigerator, but the noise had gotten louder since he arrived.

"Oh, the refrigerator? It's not new but it works fine. Only, it didn't make any noise back in New York. Do you think it needs time to settle?"

"No, I don't think it's going to get better on its own. Do you want me to take a look while I'm here?" asked Lou.

Lou finished cleaning the dishwasher powder from the floor, and pulled out the fridge for inspection.

"Looks like they bolted down the compressor for the trip out west. I'll just loosen it here for you and see if it quiets down," Lou said. He loosened the bolts and the jarring noise stopped.

"You're a genius Lou, thank you!" Maria eagerly expressed her gratitude between bites of orange segments.

"Sure, no problem," he said. Before replacing the fridge he asked, "Is it difficult for you to open the door from this side?" Lou noticed the door opened next to an island cabinet.

"I don't know why the door opens like that; it never got in the way in New York."

"Well, I can change the door to swing the other way if you want."

"You can do that? Oh, that would be so much better. Sometimes I get stuck between the cabinet and the refrigerator."

Lou kept his amusement hidden and re-hinged the door so it cleared the cabinet when the door was open.

While Lou cleaned up and wrote out the bill, Maria made him a sandwich, and insisted he stop by the next time he was in the neighborhood. She wanted her husband to meet him. Lou got into his truck and drove down the long driveway. He looked into his rear view mirror and saw Maria waving goodbye until he reached the main road.

Lou felt proud of himself. He realized the last two jobs required no special skill but the customers had been so grateful. He felt like a Canadian Rocky saving the damsel in distress on the train tracks. He took a bite out of the sandwich Maria gave him.

Two down, one to go, Lou set course to deliver his first refrigerator sale. The address was in an unincorporated part of the County. The closer he got, the bumpier the roads became from lack of maintenance. Lou was glad he had strapped the fridge into the truck so well. He worried the potholes he drove over would cause a flat tire but at least the appliance would arrive in good condition.

Old man Rick was happy to see the truck, which was now covered in a fine dust, arrive. Throughout the installation, he and Lou talked and laughed as if they were old friends. Rick had been a plumber before he retired. They swapped vicious guard dog stories. They exchanged opinions on which league would produce Superbowl champs.

"Hey, how about a cup of joe?" Rick asked.

"Sure, you're my last stop, why not? You know, I hope you don't mind me saying this but we talk to each other like we're the same age."

"Well, thanks, my ex-wife used to tell me I was immature too."

"Yeah, you really need to grow up," Lou countered which made Rick laugh. "You know, I kind of feel guilty for using my magic on you," Lou said honestly.

"What magic, you got some kind of voodoo?"

"Nah, I'm just a superior salesperson that's all. I knew the guarantee would seal the deal."

"So, I guess you'll replace the fridge when it breaks eh?" Rick asked.

"Sure, you've got a back up coming to you some day."

The old man laughed and said, "I don't want to burst your bubble, but I almost didn't buy the fridge because at my age, what do I need a lifetime guarantee for? I wanted a rebate!"

They continued bantering which made Lou wish he and his Dad had the same rapport. "Oh! Hey, sorry to cut this short, I forgot about my Dad. I'm his ride and he's probably ready to go home."

Rick looked disappointed. "Yeah, tgif, and all that. Have a good weekend, kid."

Lou rushed out of the house and into the fog that had rolled in on the afternoon breeze.

Twenty-three

DEBRIEF

MONDAY morning at the shop, Frank savored his coffee and read the Daily Journal. He was procrastinating. He had promised himself that when he got to work, he would inform Lou that Mrs. Faxon had called to compliment him for "fixing" her washer. Frank planned to tell Lou he was impressed he had resolved the problem diplomatically. Instead, he was scanning the paper.

Suddenly, Frank grabbed the reading glasses he was wearing to be sure he was seeing clearly. Evidently, while he was closing up shop last Thursday, a robbery had occurred not far from where he sat. And, it involved someone he knew well.

"Lou! Get in here, Lou!"

Lou was dusting appliances in the showroom. The tone of his dad's voice made him drop the feather duster and run to the office.

"Have you seen this?" Frank asked, pointing to the headline 'Brazen Jewelry Store Heist.'

"No, Pop. Hey! That looks like Dar's shop in the photo," Lou said.

"It is! Listen, 'San Elmos Police are looking for a man and woman whom they say robbed a jewelry store

123

at gunpoint Thursday at around five in the evening. The suspects stole a single, 8 carat diamond which the owner, Dar Hassanpour, had planned to cut into separate diamonds. According to Officer Jim Geraghty with San Elmos Police, 'an unidentified man holding a handgun approached the counter where Hassanpour was helping a woman posing as the gunman's fiancée. (The robber) gave directions to the owner, but we don't have any information indicating any threats were made,' Geraghty said. No shots were fired and the owner was not injured.'"

"Thank God," Frank said and continued reading, "'Employees of other stores on Broadway did not see the robbery occur or anything unusual. Anyone with any information on the crime is advised to call the San Elmos Police.' I've got to talk to Dar," Frank said dismayed. The phone rang.

"Good Morning, Clean and Cold Appliances," Frank answered.

"Well, good morning to you," said a male voice with a strong New York accent, honeyed with sarcasm.

"I'd like to speak to the manager please."

"Yes Sir, this is Frank." Frank did not reveal his owner status because he got more information from the customer incognito. Besides, something in the tone of this caller's voice made Frank feel cautious.

"Well, *Frank*, did you send one of your boys out to Franklin Valley last Friday to fix my dishwasher?"

"Yes, sir. We did have a service call out there to fix a dishwasher. Is this Mr. Gutierrez?"

"Yes. Finally, I found the right shop. Mind telling me how your boy managed to break my refrigerator?" Mr. Gutierrez said. "

124

Frank looked over at his son who was slouched contentedly in his chair. He sent Lou to fix a dishwasher at the old Hallidie Chateau. Had he done something to the refrigerator?

Mr. Gutierrez continued, "I've gone all weekend without my fridge and you had better get somebody out here with some know-how ASAP."

Frank had almost complimented Lou on his service calls. He realized it was foolish to praise his son before he had all the facts.

"Mr. Gutierrez, would you please hold on a moment while I put the technician on the phone?" Frank put his hand over the mouthpiece.

"Uh, Lou. Remember the dishwasher you fixed Friday?" Frank asked, with a twang of condescension and a penetrating look.

"Yeah, sure Dad," Lou answered, feeling his face turn red because compliments embarrassed him and that is what he expected. He remembered how much he had helped Mrs. Gutierrez last Friday.

"Good. Well, the owner of the home, Mr. Gutierrez, would like to talk to you. Something about a refrigerator he says you broke." Frank relinquished the phone without removing his piercing gaze. Lou took the receiver, disoriented by his Dad's message and demeanor.

"Hello Mr. Gutierrez, this is Lou, did I hear something about a broken refrigerator?" Lou asked.

"Something about that, yes. I've been without a refrigerator all weekend and I'm getting tired of talking about it!"

"Well, isn't it cold inside the fridge?" Lou asked, incredulous he had damaged the appliance.

"How the hell should I know? I can't open the damn thing! I'm hungry, I'm thirsty, the refrigerator has stopped running, and you were the last one to touch it!"

With a wink at his Dad, Lou took his free hand and covered his mouth to suppress a laugh. Frank wrinkled his brow at his son's sudden mirth.

"Sir, didn't your wife mention I fixed the fridge?" Lou asked.

"My wife left for Cowboy Camp and left me with the fridge you BROKE," Mr. Gutierrez corrected loudly. Lou moved the phone a few inches from his ear.

"OK, I think I understand the problem now, just bear with me one more minute Mr. Gutierrez. The fridge might not sound like it is running as usual because I unbolted the compressor. So, it's not making noise but it's still working. A motor in a nice fridge like yours shouldn't make any noise at all. Now, would you please do me a favor and try pulling open the fridge door from the side opposite from the one you usually open? I switched the door swing for you so the door had more room to open." There was no response so after awhile Lou asked, "How does it feel in there? Cold enough?"

"Cold enough? Yeah, I have to admit it is. There's beer in here ... and some casseroles my wife made me ... and some of my favorite Chardonnay. I guess I'll be eating humble pie for dinner. Next time you're around come on up and I'll pour you a glass of my finest wine."

"Ah, thanks Mr. Gutierrez, that sounds nice."

"Sure kid, OK, well, have a good day now. Sorry to bother you." Mr. Gutierrez said.

"No worries, and say hello to Mrs. Gutierrez for me." Lou hung up the phone still grinning at his Dad.

Lou explained the service call and Frank's expression uncurled from dismayed confusion to animated relief. Maybe he had been right to trust Lou. He had often told Mae that operator error made up many of his calls

He reached out and put his hand on Lou's shoulder appreciatively, "Lou, I want you to know how…" The phone rang, interrupting Frank. Lou, however, continued to watch his father's mouth expectantly like a desert dweller looked to the sky for rain.

Twenty-Four

THIEF

"JUST GO." Eleanor wished she could run to the beat of her heart but she walked in a deliberate, measured pace instead. She wondered if the pounding of her pulse in her ears was audible to passersby. She hoped the cold, scattered drizzle would camouflage the beads of sweat forming and dripping from her temples.

"Just go," she told herself, "Just go." The eight carat diamond was light but it felt heavy in her jean jacket pocket. She imagined it glared like a bright beacon.

"Just go." Her back burned with imaginary eyes, her ears rang with imaginary footsteps.

"Just go. Do not run. One more block ..." and she could slip into her apartment.

She arrived at the front door, unprepared. Adrenaline plumped her fingers, frustrating her efforts to remove the key from the back pocket of her tight jeans. Finally, she got the key out and inserted it into the front door. She hustled through the lobby and into the dark hall. Her veins warmed with relief; the laundry room was empty. She opened the middle dryer and cursed the loud latch. She slid the lint trap out of its track, licked the giant gem, and dropped it down the lint

128

chute. She replaced the trap, and shut the dryer door. Unobserved, she darted out the back exit, into the wet gloom.

Twenty-Five

MONEY PIT

"NOW WHAT ... Hello, Clean and Cold Appliance, how can I help you?"

"Hey Frank, it's me, Jay Bicho."

"Oh, hey Jay, haven't heard from you for awhile." Not a bad thing, Frank thought.

"Yeah, well, Bob said I could call, I don't like to bother him too often with this stuff; he's a big, busy, business man you know. I've got a list here are you ready?" Jay said flippantly.

Frank rolled his eyes in frustration before taking down the four orders. Frank would have to warn Lou about how Jay Bicho waited too long to call for repairs. The tenants blamed the repairman for enduring weeks of broken appliances. The worse thing about Jay's jobs was his apartments were filled with vermin, like cockroaches and rats.

"OK Jay, we'll be out there this afternoon." Frank hung up and sighed. He and Jay had opposite views of work. Frank's effort was the same for people of every status. According to Mae, he tried even harder for those of lower status. He wanted to help the tenants in Jay's building, most of whom were hardworking, but who would never catch up in the rat race. Jay's effort was in direct proportion to a person's status: little status, little effort.

After lunch, Lou and Frank grabbed their toolboxes and closed up the shop. Going out the back door, Frank locked the knob, then the bolt, and met Lou in the truck. Frank used the short drive over to Main Street to prepare Lou for the vermin and poverty to which he would be exposed.

"Remember, Lou. If they could, these people would live like you and I. Treat them like you would anyone else."

They parked in the loading zone in front of the Bicho Apartments, and split up the work orders, two each. When they arrived, a departing tenant held the door for them. Frank went directly to the stairwell, and up to the third floor apartment with a fridge problem.

Lou found the laundry room by the lobby. First, he scanned the coin operated washers and dryers. Next, he noticed a woman adorned with large hair curlers. She sat on a stackable chair near the first washer.

"Hello M'am," Lou said. The woman glared at him. Her arms were folded, her legs were crossed, and her slippered foot bobbed to the beat of a dryer. Lou ignored her snub and scanned the service order for the broken appliance. He knelt in front of a dryer just as the woman demanded, "You fixin' that thing?"

"Yes I am, M'am," Lou said.

"Well you better give me my damn money back. That thing ate up my quarters and I want 'em back," she said pointing accusingly at the dryer.

"Oh, well, OK. They said the dryer wasn't drying," he said.

"I know it don't dry, that's what I'm telling you. It don't *work*, but I did not know that until *after* I put my quarters in. Now how come it ain't too broken to take my quarters, but it's too broken to dry my clothes?"

"That's a good question M'am. Let me take a look OK?"

The woman harrumphed back to her chair, and Lou resumed his exploration. In the belly of the machine, he discovered a bra had bound up the pulleys. This was not good because a bound motor would run hot; hot enough to seize up. He uncoiled the bra and pulled it loose from the machine.

"Excuse me M'am. If you use this dryer, perhaps this bra is yours?"

The woman stood, walked up to Lou, ripped the garment from his outstretched hand, and stomped out of the laundry room. It occurred to him that she should be grateful to get her bra back but he shrugged it off. Everyone has a bad day.

He got back to work and finally discovered the problem with the dryer was as he suspected. Though usually supportive, the bra had burnt out the motor. Now a decision must be made, replace or repair? Frank had taught him the formula for making this decision. If the cost of the part was more than fifty percent of the appliance, replacement was the best option.

A new motor was indeed much more than half the value of a new machine. So, Lou would recommend that Jay buy a new appliance. He taped up the coin slots and marked the dryer "out of order" in anticipation of it being junked. Meanwhile, Frank was arguing with a woman upstairs.

"Mrs. White, how did you end up with holes in your refrigerator in the first place?" he asked.

"I was teaching my son a lesson. He been takin' too much money from me and I found out what he was buying. I raised him all by myself and I love him. I can't see him poisoning himself with those drugs. I wouldn't give him no more money and he tried to scare me that's all. Shootin' behind me, fool ..." she said.

"Your son shot the refrigerator ..."

"Yes, that's right. He was tryin' to scare me but I wouldn't give him no more money. No way, no how. But you got to fix this refrigerator for me because my milk's gone bad and I can't keep nothin' cold," she said.

Frank thought for a minute and remembered Mae's admiration of single mothers. She considered them brave soldiers who protected their families when others deserted.

"Look, Mrs. White, I'll talk to Mr. Jay about getting you a new fridge. I can't fix this one today, I'm sorry."

The woman followed Frank out of her apartment demanding, "What am I'm gonna do with this spoilt milk? How long am I gonna have to wait now?"

Frank tried to assure her he would get her a new refrigerator soon, but she returned to her apartment and slammed her front door in frustration.

He met Lou on the stairs and together they climbed to the fourth floor. In one flight of steps, Lou debriefed his Dad about the burnt out dryer. They agreed the dryer would be scrapped. They parted ways at the top of the stairwell. Lou went to the right and knocked on the door of apartment 401.

"Whose it is?"

"Appliance Man, Sir."

A small man cracked open the door revealing one eye, then opened it wide revealing the rest of his hunched body. He escorted Lou with shuffled steps to the lifeless refrigerator in the kitchen.

"My refrigerator, she no work," he said sadly.

"Third refrigerator in three days, how 'bout that?" Lou asked affably. "Don't worry; I'll get her working again for you."

He pulled out the refrigerator. Then, as if hit by a shock wave, Lou jumped a foot in the air and onto a nearby stool. He stared wide eyed at a roiling sea of black insects where the fridge had been.

"Cucaracha ..." the man rasped.

"Whoah! I did not expect that! Sir, maybe I could come back another time," Lou said backing off the stool and inching out of the kitchen.

"No! Just minute!" the man said. He rushed passed Lou out of the kitchen. Seconds later, he returned with a can of hairspray in one hand and a lighter in the other. He pointed the can at the black mass and lit the spray with his lighter. A stream of fire rained down on the bugs like Armageddon. Lou had heard roaches could survive nuclear war, but evidently they were no match for hairspray. The spectacle rendered Lou immobile, but not speechless.

"Look, Sir, I can't work back there behind your fridge ..." Lou said.

"Just minute!" the man said. He swiftly swept up the crispy carcasses with two pieces of cardboard. When he finished sweeping, he revealed a toothless smile under sparkling eyes. Lou relented, returned the smile, and rolled his sleeves up to work. He ignored the phantom, creepy crawly sensations on his back and neck.

Frank's call was not going much better. He knocked on the door of apartment 411 where three pairs of little brown eyes and one pair of tired ones greeted him and paraded him to the kitchen.

"Sir, I have a weird problem. Something smells like burnt hair when I wash my dishes," explained the busy mother of three. The children pranced around Frank's toolbox until their mother shooed them out of the kitchen. Frank smelled the odor too and searched under the sink for the source.

He aimed the beam of his flashlight into the dark back corner where he discovered a ball of fur. Looking closer, he could see the varmint was stuck behind some exposed electric wire. A rodent could be infected with rabies, so he used the handle of a large screwdriver to kill and bring the beast out of its last resting place.

"Oh! Henry!" the mother gasped. She explained, "Henry was the family hamster, he disappeared a week ago but I guess we found him."

"Oh, I'm so sorry, please forgive me," Frank begged.

"No, no, no, don't feel bad. To be honest with you, I was relieved when he disappeared. I didn't realize the costs of having another mouth to feed, even a tiny one. I have to keep this from the children anyway. When he escaped, I told them he moved to a restaurant where other hamsters played and they could eat all they wanted. They begged me for another hamster but we don't have the money. Besides, whose pet is it after they get tired of it? Mine!" she said emphatically.

Frank smiled and remembered how Mae had said the same thing. Lou had begged her for a hermit crab. Frank teased her when she worried if the crab was eating enough. Of course, for them a pet was an accessory, but for this little family it was a sacrifice.

"Well, let's call this our little secret then. I'll smuggle him out in my toolbox, OK? No charge today."

The mother called her children who followed Frank in a farewell procession shouting happy goodbyes and thank yous.

Lou and Frank met in front of Jay's apartment door. "Are you going to say something to him about this place? If he's the manager, isn't he supposed to take care of these people's apartments? I can't believe he lets people live this way!"

It was getting harder for Frank to contain his own frustration with Jay. He slid the service bills under Jay's door.

Twenty-six

WHAT FRIENDS ARE FOR

THE NEXT MORNING, Lou and Frank discussed the jobs at the Bicho apartment over coffee. No surprise, they were interrupted by the ring of the phone.

"Good Morning, Clean and Cold Appliance, how can I help you?" Frank said.

"I need to talk to the manager," a gruff female voice demanded.

"Yes M'am, this is Frank."

"Frank, this is Tanesha and I got some advice for you. Fire the fool you sent over here yesterday," she said plainly.

"Hello, Tanesha. I'm sorry, can you tell me where it was that I sent that fool?"

"Main Street! This fool couldn't get my money back from the dryer."

Frank looked at Lou. He had not mentioned a problem with any of the Bicho tenants. Maybe they should have done the service calls together. He should have observed Lou's behavior before sending him out alone.

"Oh, I'm sorry to hear that. The manager, Jay Bicho, takes the money out of the coin boxes so he should be able to get your money back," Frank said.

"Jay won't give me nothin, but I don't care about the money anyway. The problem is, this fool hands me a teeny, tiny bra and asks me if it's mine. Any fool can see it's too small to be mine. He had to be joking, or blind. Now which do you think it was?"

Frank paused. Diplomacy would be needed here. Was Lou blind, in which case he could not see the woman? Or, was he joking, in which case he had a very inappropriate sense of humor? How did Lou get himself in these sticky situations? He had cautioned Lou about talking to the customers. In all of Frank's years of repair, he had never experienced a problem like this one.

"M'am, if I understand correctly, my repairman thought that he was giving you back your bra after it had gotten tangled in the dryer. But actually, he was giving you a bra that did not belong to you..."

"And was too small!" she interjected.

"...and was too small to be yours. Do I have that correct?"

"Yes, that's exactly what happened. I just don't know how he could make such a mistake," she said, sincerely disturbed.

"Please accept our apologies M'am, because you know what? You're right. The repairman *is* practically blind. He needs glasses to see clearly, and he forgot them yesterday. I'll make sure he wears them next time. We were certainly in error, yes M'am." Frank was a proponent of untruths if they brought peace to a situation.

"Well why didn't you say so? That explains it, he *is* blind. You have a good day now," she said and hung up. Frank hung up too and regarded his son. Working with the public required a lot of sensitivity. Working

138

with women's lingerie required even more sensitivity. Mae would have known what to say to Lou about the bra situation. Why, he grieved, had she left him when he still needed her?

"Did you talk to Dar yet?" Lou asked, sensing a change of topic was in order.

"Yeah, we met at the Coffee Shop. He was pretty shook up about the robbery. He said the robbers looked like any engaged couple except the guy was older. He closed the shop and was about to put the diamond in his safe when the robbers knocked on his door."

"Did they have a gun?"

"Dar wasn't sure about that. He said the guy kept a hand in his pocket the whole time. Even so, Dar's lucky to be alive. Lou, I have to call Jay and Exelda. Why don't you go over the inventory orders?" Frank abruptly dismissed Lou and dialed Jay's number.

"Hello, this is Jay."

"Jay this is Frank, I'm sending over a new refrigerator to 311, and I'll ask Exelda to scrap the old one. And we need to scrap the coin dryer in the laundry room. It's got a burnt out motor. I'll order another one but it probably won't get here for two weeks."

"OK, Frank, that's fine, just send me the invoices like usual. I don't think Bob's going to like all these new appliances, but he trusts you for some reason." Jay did not mention the generous appliance fund his brother provided, or that he helped himself to it.

"I'll send my guys over to pick up the new fridge tomorrow," Jay offered.

"No, thanks Jay, Lou will drop it off," Frank said.

This was the first time Frank had refused these deliveries. Jay quickly recalled how Frank had accused him of using free labor. Jay surmised it was natural for laborers to stick together, but the lack of respect Frank demonstrated was insulting. He felt he deserved gratitude for allowing those pathetic people to stay in his building. Some day, he would put Frank in his place.

Frank, not one for small talk, gave the usual curt goodbye and clicked off the line. He had little respect for Jay, and he wondered how he would keep his self respect *and* his biggest customer happy.

Next, Frank called Exelda. He explained how the dryer motor had burnt out, and how Mrs. White's son had riddled her refrigerator with bullets in an effort to extort money from her.

"Sure, we can pick up the bra burnt dryer and the holy fridge right away!" Exelda responded. Frank was grateful he had such reliable business partners, but their relationship went deeper than business.

In the beginning, Lamar was wary of doing business with unfamiliar people, specifically unfamiliar white people. Frank was careful too and recorded every transaction between them. Their relationship was professional but guarded.

Everything changed when Exelda began fundraising for her community's new church. An earthquake had damaged the hall they used for services. Paint peeled on cracked walls. Cracked walls revealed insecure beams. The people needed a safe, secure space to meet.

Lamar discouraged Exelda from fundraising. He thought fundraising was glorified begging. It was beneath a niece of his. He thought donors would want control in exchange for their money, especially the white donors. Also, he feared a personal request for money would hurt their business with Frank. Exelda persisted, however. The church, she decided, was more important than business, power, or her ego, and she asked Frank for a donation.

Frank did not answer immediately. He was fine with the request, but he and Mae made financial decisions together. Frank asked Mae about the donations while they washed dinner dishes one evening. When Mae heard what the money was for, she was enthusiastic. Mae was Catholic, and she knew the money was for a Baptist church. Mae reasoned that if Exelda came from that church, it must be worth supporting.

Frank wrote so many checks over the years, he felt like the new church was his too. He even re-wrote checks after thieves stole from an unlocked collection basket. Finally, the building was completed and the pastor organized a large celebration. Frank and Mae squeezed into the packed church. They were the only white people at the church except for one white woman in one of the farthest pews. Frank did not know her but felt connected to her. At that moment, he understood how Lamar felt in groups of white people.

"It's late, Exelda. Why don't you and Lamar pick up the machines tomorrow? Lou is going to deliver the new refrigerator in the afternoon; you can back him up if the bra lady gets after him."

Exelda laughed and said, "Yeah, and he can back me up if I run into that boy who almost iced his Mama for drug money."

They both laughed nervously before saying goodbye.

Twenty-seven

LOST AND FOUND... AND LOST

ELEANOR'S nerves were frayed. Charles had stayed away from her since the robbery. She missed him and his protective arms. She dreaded the walk to work; especially when police patrols drove slowly passed her. She knew the diamond was safe in the dryer downstairs but it felt good to confirm it occasionally.

The laundry room was unoccupied, thankfully, when she arrived. She squinted her eyes at the floor between two of the coin dryers. On the floor was a black stain, in the shape of a square. It was strange she had not noticed it earlier. She opened one of the dryer doors and lifted the lint tray out of its track. She peered inside with a pen light. The space was empty. She had probably dropped the diamond in the other dryer.

Again, she peered inside the lint space of the other dryer. Again, she saw no glint of the huge diamond. Again, she squinted at the black stain on the floor, between the two dryers.

"I'm glad I didn't give up looking! What are you doing down here, my little pet?" Ricky said, startling Evelyn.

"Shit, you scared me. What are you doing here?"

"Bitch. Don't talk to me that way. Give me my money and I'll go."

"Your money? Ricky, I told you, I need time. You told me you wouldn't be back for awhile!" Evelyn said. Suddenly an arm reached around Ricky's neck.

Charles grabbed a hold of Ricky and whispered in his ear, "I have something for you." Inserting a knife through Ricky's jacket and nicking the flesh under his ribs, Charles encouraged Ricky forward and through the back door of the laundry room. Once outside he forced Ricky against the wall and bared his teeth.

"She is mine, mine alone. If I see you around her again, I will ram up this knife so far your eyes will bleed." Charles removed his sharpened point, and Ricky scampered off holding his side.

Suddenly, regret seized Charles. Perhaps he should have removed Ricky from the situation permanently. Eleanor might be tempted, or coerced, to share her sudden bounty with him. Charles ruefully realized he would need to plug the crack in his armor.

He went back into the laundry room, but Evelyn was gone.

Twenty-eight

JULIA

LOU AND FRANK ate their cereal in silence. Usually loquacious, Lou was thoughtful. He thought that working with his Dad would fill a void in his heart that remained despite the work. He considered the crunchy squares of wheat drenched in cold milk.

Frank liked the peace but not the meal. They ate cold breakfast regularly now that Mae was gone. They knew how to cook, but the kitchen felt lonely without Mae. The cupboards were stocked with boxes and cans of prepared meals.

"Lou, today is going to be pretty busy. Four calls came in yesterday afternoon and you've got to get them all done this morning because in the afternoon, you need to get down to the Bichos and deliver a new refrigerator to Mrs. White on the third floor. She's the one whose son shot up her refrigerator. Be careful, in case he's around. Exelda and Lamar will have picked up her old fridge by the time you get there."

"OK, what's happening this morning?" Lou got up and put his bowl and coffee mug in the sink.

"Hey, there's no maid around here, put your dishes in the dishwasher. The Convent called and they need some work done. And, an old buddy called. He's moving out of his place on Delaware and he wants us to buy his old refrigerator. He's almost moved out, just go in and take the refrigerator. Oh, you're going to the Highlands too. No one is home there either, but the lady will leave the door unlocked. Make sure you lock it when you leave. The last one is for a nice, old customer in Hillswood, also not home." Frank got up and put his bowl and mug in the dishwasher.

"I've never been to the Convent before," Lou said nervously. He knew his Dad worked gratis for the Sisters but he had never joined him. It was a strange idea that sisters existed outside a classroom. Even stranger, they had dirty dishes and laundry.

"It's a piece of cake. You just gotta find the service entrance on the south side of the building. Those sisters are a bunch of characters, I tell you. Oh, and make sure you plan your route. You've gotta drive all over the peninsula this morning and you will waste time if you have to backtrack."

Lou dropped his Dad off at the shop. Frank had placed the four work orders in four pockets of an accordion file. He instructed Lou to keep all the paperwork for each job separate, reminded him about the one way streets at Poplar, and warned him again about choosing his route carefully.

Lou got on Highway 101 and was relieved to see the heavier traffic going south. Having no one to talk to, he switched the radio from his Dad's AM talk station to an FM classic rock broadcast. He tried to keep his eyes on the lanes but stole glimpses in the direction of the airport. In the blue horizon, he watched pairs of planes, like majestic, stiff winged dragons, descend to their landings.

146

On the street in front of the Convent address, Lou rechecked his map to be sure he was in the right place. Oak trees lined the long driveway to what looked like a mansion, not a Convent. The address was correct. So, he drove up and parked next to the main manor.

He remembered his tools, found the side entrance his Dad had described, and rang the bell. A tall, middle aged sister opened the door and introduced herself. She wore khakis, a white t-shirt, penny loafers and dangly earrings. Sisters had changed a lot since Lou was a kid. She led Lou down the hall to the laundry room. He took one step inside and stopped cold.

He could not believe his eyes. There, in the corner, stood a beauty he had seen in magazines but never in person. The light shaft from the window vents, which were positioned high along the far wall, hit her just below the belly and Lou was compelled to kneel in front of her for a better look.

"I can't believe it; I've never seen one that had a motor. *Where* did this *come* from, Sister?" Lou asked.

"She's a beauty all right. We can't bring ourselves to get rid of her, even though we don't use her anymore. Years ago, one of the Sisters came from a farm in Gilroy, and brought it with her. They didn't have electricity on their farm so the gas motor came in handy. It's a 1935 Maytag wringer washer and it still works! I don't know how to use it, but our aide Julia keeps it running," Sister Martha explained.

Suddenly, out of the darkness of another hallway, a woman appeared. The light from the window vents shone on her face. It was Julia.

"Oh good! I was afraid I'd miss the repair." Julia was breathless and looked relieved to see Lou.

"Sister Martha, Mother Superior would like to see you when you're available," she added.

"Uh oh, that means right now. I'd better go. Lou, This is the aide I was telling you about, who runs the old machinery, and helps our retired Sisters get around. Julia, this is Lou,"

"It's nice to see you, again," Julia said.

"You too, I'm Lou. It's nice to see you, Julia," Lou said.

Julia smiled and said, "Yes, I know you're Lou. Sister, Lou's mother and my mother were in the Garden Club together. I'm so sorry about your Mom, Lou. She was so nice, and an excellent baker too." Lou smiled at the memory of his Mom's cooking.

"Thanks, I really miss her. Sorry about your Mom too, Julia. I know my Mom liked her a lot."

The moment Lou realized he was having an easy conversation with Julia was the moment he faltered, as if he just noticed he was suspended in mid air with no means of staying aloft. Lou blushed and looked down at the laces crisscrossing his work boots. Sister Martha coughed, and Lou remembered the only competition for Julia's beauty in the room.

"Oh! I almost forgot! Julia, Sister said you knew how to work this old Maytag." Lou turned toward the washer. Sister Martha was growing uneasy. Mother Superior was waiting.

"Sure, would you like me to start it for you?" Julia asked.

Sister rolled her eyes. How could she leave this attractive young couple in a room full of appliances, alone? Julia checked the gas tank and pumped air into the tank with the foot pedal until the motor began to

148

rumble. Lou opened the lid and delighted at the back and forth motion of the agitator.

"If we filled her up, we could get some habits washed and wrung, Sister," Julia shouted over the motor.

"Maybe we should be on our way and let Lou get to work. He must be busy," Sister Martha yelled. Julia switched off the old Maytag and Lou turned to inspect the large modern washer behind them.

"Is this the washer that needs fixing?" he asked.

"Yes, it is Lou. Well, thank you so much, we'd best be moving along now. Julia?" Sister wiped her brow. She opened her arm in the direction of the hallway, and Mother Superior.

"Thanks Sister, but I'm going to watch Lou fix the washer," Julia said.

It took a moment for Sister to digest this intention. She knew Julia had learned a lot from watching Lou's father work, but this boy was her age. Finally, the call of Mother Superior outweighed her present concerns

"All righty, then. Don't worry, I'll be right back. I could be back any minute even!"

Lou watched Sister Martha leave and then looked at Julia who stood with her hands on her hips. No thoughts came to mind so Lou silently pulled off the cover of the washer. Immediately he saw the problem. Julia did too.

"Oh! That's easy, all we have to do is replace the belt," she said. Lou looked back at her stunned.

"That's right! How did you know that?" he asked.

"I guess I've learned a little by watching your Dad work. We really appreciate how much he does for our Sisters. I thought that if I learned enough, I could do some of our own repairs. Do you mind me shadowing you?"

"No, I don't mind, Julia, but if you learn too much, I won't be able to come back," he teased.

"Well, that's the idea!" Julia said. Lou raised his eyebrows in disappointment, and Sister Martha popped back into the washroom.

"Julia, Mother asks if you'll help the Sisters down to lunch."

"Oh. Sure, I'll be right there, Sister. Well, thanks for coming by, Lou. It was nice seeing you," Julia said. She turned and dashed passed Sister Martha and out of the laundry room.

"Lou, is there anything I can do for you?"

"No, Sister, thanks. I have the part in my truck. I'll let myself back in and fix the washer in no time." He smiled at Sister Martha. She smiled back and disappeared quietly into the dark hallway.

Lou continued to look at the empty doorway. He wished he could follow Julia. He looked at the old Maytag and remembered how she had pumped the pedal until the motor came clamoring to life. The new belt for the washer was in the truck. It would take him a minute to get it and come back. But something about the room, or maybe the warm morning light shining in it, made him not want to leave, even for a minute.

Frank had written 'no bill' on the service order for the Sisters. So, after Lou got the washer working again, he cleaned up and got back on El Camino.

He drove south to the soon to be sold home of Frank's old friend where Lou would find the refrigerator to pick up. The address was missing on the order but his Dad had told him it was the third house from the corner on Poplar and Delaware. He found the house but no parking place for his truck. So, he parked in the house driveway.

Lou was uncomfortable about going into someone's vacant home so he called through the front door, "Appliance Man!" the way he had observed his Dad do in similar circumstances. Frank never wanted to catch a homeowner unaware. It would leave a bad impression and jeopardize his business with them. As expected, the house was quiet. He proceeded through the front rooms.

Feeling like Goldilocks, he noticed his Dad's friend still had a lot to move. There was a couch, comfortable looking chairs and even knick knacks. He found the kitchen and prepared to move the refrigerator. Unfortunately, there was food left inside which Lou had to empty onto the kitchen table.

"What do you think you're doing?" said a voice from the doorway. Lou turned to see a woman clothed only in a towel.

"Uh, excuse me M'am, I thought you moved out," Lou said surprised.

"Excuse me?" the woman said.

"I'm with Clean and Cold Appliances. You sold us your refrigerator?" Lou said.

In response, she grabbed a head of lettuce from the table and hurled it over his head. Unhappy with her aim she followed the lettuce with cups of yogurt, a bottle of mustard, relish, an olive jar and other groceries Lou could not identify because he was ducking and covering his head.

"Wait! What? Hey!" was all he could muster between missiles. Since she was unwilling to listen, he turned and escaped from the house. Quickly backing his truck out of the driveway, Lou pondered the woman's reaction. Maybe she was not happy about the move, but did she have to take it out on him? He gave her some her some credit, though. Despite her significant exertion, she had kept the towel on. It never occurred to Lou he had gone into the wrong house.

There were two more calls. When he saw the Hillswood address on the next order to fix a broken dishwasher, he realized his mistake. It was north, in the direction of the Convent. He should have gone there first. Now, he would be later than his dad expected. Even more distressing, he had forgotten his lunch.

Traffic had gotten bad on the freeway, Lou was hungry, and his mood was starting to sour. The next service call was to a home with yet another absent owner. What if they forgot to leave the house open?

Lou took the exit for the exclusive town of Hillswood. There were no average homes in Hillswood, only huge homes cloaked behind mature trees or vine covered walls.

Once he found the correct address, he drove through the property, catching glimpses of the looming abode between tree limbs. He lugged his toolbox, up the marble steps and stopped at the forged iron and glass door. He turned the knob. To Lou's relief, the door was unlocked.

He shouted "Appliance Man!" a bit louder than usual, then listened. The only response was his echo which bounced off the spiraling staircase.

He shouted a second time, more for the fun of hearing his echo than out of necessity. The kitchen was easy to find and he set to work on the broken dishwasher. When he removed the front panel, he heard shuffling behind him. Not again, he thought.

"Sir, stand up slowly and put your hands where I can see them," the officer said. Lou went cold and clammy. He cooperated with the request.

"How did you enter the house today, Sir?" the officer asked.

"The owner left the door open so I could fix the washer."

The officer looked skeptical. "Really? Well, if the owner was expecting you, probably she should have turned off the house alarm, don't you think, Sir? It certainly looks like you're here to fix the dishwasher but I'm going to have to contact the owner before I can let this go."

The security officer dialed an emergency phone number for the owner's daughter.

"Oh! I'm so sorry! My mother must have forgotten to turn off the security alarm but we definitely called Clean and Cold to come over today. It's perfectly all right for them to be in the house alone. We've known the owner for years." Lou was exonerated.

The officer relaxed. "I'll be on my way then, Lou. Sorry for the trouble. We can't be too careful in my line of work. Hey, you should write a book. I bet a lot of strange things happen in your business," the officer said before leaving.

Right then, Lou could not imagine anyone wanting to read about his crummy life. His nerves were frayed and his fingers shook while he finished the repair. He ran the dishwasher, cleaned up, and left a copy of the bill on the kitchen counter by the phone.

In the truck, he pulled out the accordion file and reviewed his job assignments. He was already behind schedule because he had had to backtrack, and the security problem at the Hillswood home had made him later. He closed the accordion file. His stomach growled. He rifled through the glove compartment for an old protein bar.

When he finished eating, he felt better. He remembered his Mom saying that everyone falls, what matters is getting up from the fall. Sooner or later, he would find Success Street around the corner of Failure Avenue. Renewed in body and spirit, Lou drove to one of his favorite neighborhoods on earth.

Twenty-nine

HOT DOG

LOU checked the rear view mirror for police. He knew he was innocent, but could not shake the guilty feeling he had developed in the Hillswood kitchen.

Plus, he had suspicions of his own. He was on his way to another service call involving an absent owner. Had his father given him difficult jobs deliberately? Or, was it coincidence, and Lou's bad planning, so much had gone wrong?

His doubts receded on the drive up the hill to the Highlands. The Highlands was a diverse neighborhood, full of kind retired folks, kids, and dogs. When Lou was a kid, he loved to join his Dad on repair trips to this special neighborhood. Frank must have been on the neighbors' referral list because he was called up there frequently. Lou remembered sneaking tools out of his Dad's toolbox, studying them, and then quietly returning them to the box while his Dad occupied himself under the sinks of the Eichler homes.

All the homes in the Highlands were Eichlers, built in the late 1950s and early 1960s. A social engineer of sorts, Eichler sold his homes to anyone of any religion or race. He believed so strongly in this policy, he resigned from the prestigious National Association of Home Builders over their lack of support.

In Lou's home, walls met the ceiling. In Eichler homes, walls might stop a few feet short of the low sloped ceilings. When he was not watching his Dad, or looking through his tools, Lou imagined throwing a football over the kitchen wall and running into the next room to catch it.

Lou still felt like that little kid but he loved the responsibility he had now. He pulled into the neighborhood and parked in front of the home address on the work order. He waved to a neighbor trimming the flowers in her front yard and pulled out his toolbox from the truck.

Lou walked up the path to the tall door. Encouraged by no home alarm signs, he reached for the round escutcheon framed doorknob and turned it passed the latch.

That's when he heard it. Somewhere in the depths of his brain, a voice said, "Not so fast. Look, before you leap." He let go of the knob and cupped his hands against the tall window by the door. A long, shiny, hardwood hallway stretched before him.

Suddenly, a little Rat Terrier skid into view. He glided on sharp claws into the hallway like a race car entering a turn in the grand prix. When he gained traction, he charged the door. Though knee high, he barked and snarled ferociously. Lou watched agape as the dog leapt at the window. All four paws landed on the glass before the little dog twisted his torso and landed clean like a gymnast off the pommel horse.

It was difficult to think over the yaps and yelps, but Lou concentrated and focused on his options. He needed to get into the house to get the job done. The front door was not a viable entry.

Like a mirage, a childhood memory emerged of 'the dog next door.' Mae had baked a cake for their neighbor. Lou carried it to their door. No one answered the doorbell but the dog. The German Shepherd snarled and bayed at Lou who left the cake on the porch. The dog barked continuously until Lou got home, and miraculously, while he played in his backyard. From that time on, any time Lou wanted to play in his backyard, he rang the dog's doorbell first.

Armed with this memory, Lou left the terrible terrier at the front door and walked to the side gate. He waved again to the neighbor who waved back and shrugged knowingly. He discovered two empty, plastic flower pots, and banged them together.

This alerted the dog to a potentially dangerous intruder. He darted to the back of his home, hurdled through his doggie door, and dashed to the side gate.

Once the little sentinel reported for duty at the gate, Lou ran back to the front door and entered the home with his toolbox. He found the kitchen off the hardwood hallway, ran inside, and slid the pocket door shut.

The terrier was cleverer than the German Shepherd. Once he chased the intruder from the gate, he bolted back inside the house in search of the enemy. No parts were required, the dishwasher pump was just clogged. Lou ignored the cacophony on the other side of the kitchen door while he finished the job quickly. It was after he had cleaned up that he realized he needed an exit strategy.

Only a pocket door separated Lou from the now humiliated and vengeful terrier. The dog's barks echoed off of the kitchen wall which, Lou noticed nostalgically, stopped a few feet short of the ceiling. He had no football to toss, but he did have an idea.

He opened the refrigerator and discovered a new pack of hotdogs. Hoping he was not ruining the dinner menu, Lou took one hotdog out of the pack. He climbed onto a countertop and peered over the kitchen wall. The crazy man's sudden appearance silenced the startled canine. Lou broke off pieces of the hotdog, and threw them into other parts of the house.

The dog deserted the wily stranger in pursuit of the morsels. Lou grabbed his tools and escaped from the kitchen. He ran to open the front door, stopped, took a moment to lock the interior knob, and shut the door soundly.

He walked down the pathway and waved to the neighbor who gave him a congratulatory wink. He would be an hour late getting back to the shop. His dad would give a chilly reception, he thought as he licked his fingers.

Thirty

WANTED

HE GRABBED HER by the collar and roughly shoved her into the dumpster shed. With his unshaven face so close to hers, the smell of tobacco and liquor stung her nostrils like nettles.

"I've been looking for you," Charles said.

"I've been looking for you too, where have you been? I hid the diamond but I wanted to be sure you were in town before I risked getting it," Evelyn said with as much innocence and calm as she could muster.

"Where is it?" he demanded. His steely, penetrating glare made her eyes ache but she held his gaze.

"Maybe it's better if only I know, then if the cops find you ..."

He grabbed her by the neck and tightened his grasp until she rasped, "I put it somewhere safe."

He gave a last squeeze and let go. She coughed and wiped tears from her cheek with her bare shoulder.

"Tell me, *now*, where it is, or you will go quietly into this dumpster." He opened his jacket to reveal the large handle of a knife.

"I put it behind the mirror in the Coffee Shop women's room," she lied hoarsely. He pointed at a tree just outside the garbage shed and said, "Meet me at 4:30 today, under that tree. Bring the diamond, or you *will* regret ever seeing my face."

At that moment, an oblivious young woman reached between Evelyn and Charles to lift a trash bin lid.

"Oh, excuse me, I just want to throw away my gum," she said. Evelyn realized it was her chance to get away. Charles would never hurt her in front of a witness. She ran out of the dumpster shed leaving Charles and the young woman behind. Charles let her go. She would bring the diamond to him, or else.

"Hi there," the young woman greeted Charles. He had forgotten she was there but recovered quickly.

"Hi yourself, beautiful," Charles said. "Would you join me for a drink at the Coffee Shop?"

Thirty-one

KEYS

ON THE DRIVE back to the shop, Lou decided to limit the information he gave his Dad about the morning. If he whined about his work orders, his Dad might think twice about sending him on solo service calls. Lou's lack of planning, the encounter with the security officer, and the food fight with the towel lady, might overshadow what was an otherwise successful day. He would focus instead on the positive, like the 1930 wringer Maytag at the Convent.

"That you, Lou?" Frank called.

"Yeah, whew, what a morning!" Lou said.

"The Highlands owner called. Did you eat the owner's hotdogs when you were there?" Frank asked, startling Lou.

"Hotdogs? Why ... oh ..." Lou had forgotten about the hotdog. Lou hesitantly described the terrier trap. Frank knew, and disliked that dog. His son's ingenuity impressed him.

Before Frank could ask about the towel lady's refrigerator on Delaware, Lou deftly changed the subject to the old Maytag at the Convent, describing every bolt and switch. Frank grew impatient with the details.

"Head over to the Bicho Apartments. You've got to deliver the new refrigerator to 'Bullet Mama.' Oh, by the way, Jay wants to see you. He wouldn't tell me why." Jay appreciated how his secrecy irritated Frank.

Still hungry, Lou asked if his Dad was going to finish the rest of his sandwich from lunch. Frank gave him the leftover piece, and helped get the small refrigerator for the Bicho Apartment on the truck.

Lou drove over to Main Street but when he arrived at the Bicho Apartment, he found a shiny, new sedan in the loading zone. He needed the loading zone to deliver the heavy refrigerator. He parked a few blocks away and left the refrigerator in the truck.

On the walk to the apartment, he passed a chain link fence which enclosed the charred and pungent remains of a burnt out building. Black, wooden planks poked out of the ruins like scaly logs in an old campfire. Fire has a quirky habit of leaving lucky areas untouched and this time it left a brightly painted sign, 'Coffee Shop,' lying unscarred in the wreckage. Lou thought the remnant was a sign of hope in the black sea of destruction.

The sign also made Lou hungry so he bought a chocolate milk and candy bar at a 'Liquor and Lottery' store en route to the apartments. He finished both by the time he rang Jay's doorbell. Jay buzzed the front door and waited for Lou to get to his apartment.

"Lou, hey, how are you, son? Come in and sit down," Jay welcomed. His apartment was sparsely furnished with a couple of armchairs and a huge, roll top desk. The roll top housed many drawers and shelves but it was strewn with used yellow legal pads, stacked binders, file folders, and a laptop computer. A small living room window looked out at the trunk of a tree.

Lou took a seat in one of the armchairs. Normally the first to speak, Lou was reticent and uncomfortable with Jay's newfound interest in him. Also, he did not appreciate how paternal Jay behaved considering how close in age they were. He held Jay's gaze. Jay remained silent. Finally, Lou spoke.

"I couldn't deliver the refrigerator to 311 because someone was parked in the loading zone. I had to park three blocks away."

"Did you park near the burnt out place?" Jay asked.

"Yeah, I parked near there because the loading zone was blocked."

"I watched it burn. Unfortunately, the building belonged to my baby brother. He let some lowlife lease the restaurant. Then, Bob found out the place served up more than coffee so he evicted the bum tenant. We think the guy torched the place on his way out, but can't prove it. Now we're stuck with the mess, you know?" Jay said.

"Wow, that's really too bad, Jay. Did you know the tenant?"

"Everybody knows everybody around here, Lou, but that's not why I asked you to come in today. I have something important I'd like to talk to you about." He paused, looked at his watch, and then stared intently into Lou's eyes.

"Lou, I don't like to see talent wasted. I look at you and I see a talented, strong, intelligent young man. Now, I love your father like my own. So, I hate to say this, but I think he's holding you back ..." Lou tried to interrupt but Jay continued,

163

"Now just hear me out, OK? Listen, there's a lot of money available right now. Bob is buying another apartment building over in Fair Oaks. There will be a lot of work installing and maintaining all of the new appliances. We need dedicated talent. I have an idea how much you make working with your Dad. I think we could give you twice, maybe three times what he gives you. We get subsidized checks for these properties, and if we're careful with our resources, there's quite a lot of cream at the top. I want to share it with you. It's unfortunate, but if we took on your Dad too, he'd drain our share," Jay said. His offer was illegal and exaggerated but Lou believed every word.

Pleased by the open expression on Lou's face, Jay continued, "Listen, I know this is a big decision. Not everyone can handle the kind of money I'm offering you. Why don't you think about it, and get back to me?" He finished speaking but remained seated. He waited optimistically for Lou's response.

"Jay, listen. I appreciate the confidence you have in me, but you have to understand; working with my Dad is all I've ever wanted. It's never been about money. I can't separate my business from my family, it's just not possible."

Jay's countenance darkened. He tugged at the scant whiskers that grew under his pointed nose. Lou observed Jay's furrowed brow and guessed Jay usually got what he wanted. This time, Lou remained silent.

"Well, I understand fidelity to family Lou. Hell, family is everything. Why don't we say this … give it some more thought and don't rush into a decision. I'll just leave the door open for you, alright? Maybe a little extra cash will seem more attractive when you get a girlfriend, eh? Listen, to show you how much I think of you, I want you to have these." Jay held out three keys on a ring.

"Take them. They're the keys to the kingdom! One opens the front door and the others are the master keys to every apartment and closet in the building. Except my apartment of course." Jay laughed at the idea of giving his personal apartment key to Lou.

Lou looked at the keys, dumbstruck. In all of the years his Dad worked for the Bicho Brothers, Frank was never given a key to the building, let alone a master key. No one had ever put so much faith in him. Confidence ignited in Lou's gut, sparked by Jay's trust. He reached for and took the keys.

"Thank you Jay. I don't know what to say except, I will never disappoint you. I'm sorry I couldn't give you the answer you wanted to hear about your brother's new apartment though ..." Lou said.

"Let's not worry about that now, son," Jay said smiling, his mood improved. The deal had gone better than expected. Jay had assumed the crack in Frank's son's armor was greed, but he was wrong. It was only a starved ego. Affirmation was a currency he could manufacture in abundance. He stood, shook Lou's hand, and steered him triumphantly to the door.

"Uh, Jay, I need to deliver a refrigerator to 311 and the loading zone is blocked," Lou mentioned a third time.

"Oh yes, son. I parked there last night and forgot to move my car. I'll take care of that right after I lock up here. You go on ahead, and get your truck."

Lou installed the new refrigerator, and on his way out of the apartment he noticed the black, square stain in the laundry room where the coin dryer had been. Exelda and Lamar had removed the bra burnt dryer, and the shot up refrigerator from apartment 311, without the benefit of a loading zone.

Lou felt badly for them but focused on the positives. For one thing, "Bullet Mama" had offered him a tuna salad sandwich after he installed her refrigerator. Usually he refused offers of hospitality, but not having had a full lunch, Lou accepted gratefully. And, except for the food throwing towel-woman, he had accomplished a lot that day. Moreover, Jay believed in him. He walked a little taller out of the apartment building, to which he had keys.

Thirty-two

A FRIEND IN NEED

"WHITE, hot and sweet, just the way I like it," Dar said as he sipped the coffee Frank brought him.

"Dar, you've got a way with words you know that?" Frank took a sip of his coffee too.

"When you have a brush with death, you have to savor the little things, you know? I now appreciate every minute of my life."

"I'm glad they didn't hurt you Dar," Frank said in a rare revelation of affection for his old friend.

"Well, it wasn't all bad. The publicity in the paper has helped my business. I even met a new lady widow friend."

"Is that right?" Frank asked.

"Yes, and you know her. Her name is Linda Straisburg," Dar said. Frank nearly spit out his coffee.

"How does an old man like you hook a woman like that? Is it serious?" Frank asked.

"Oh yes, very much. Remember, I've got a way with words. Women cannot resist my words."

Frank put aside his personal reservations. Perhaps Linda Straisburg's insensitivity to her husband's near death experiences reflected a loveless marriage, and she really liked Dar. Dar would never believe she was a gold digger anyway. He had the look of goofy love in his eye.

"Congratulations, you old dog. She's a looker, that one. Me? I don't think I'll ever fall in love again. To be honest, I don't know what I'm living for anymore, Dar."

Dar worried about his friend. He knew how lonely he was without Mae. "Frank, you must listen to me. I have very wise words to offer you. You must realize what a difference you make here in the world."

Frank laughed. "Difference? Ha! The inventor of the washing machine made a difference. Without Mae, I don't make a difference to anyone."

"No, my friend, no. That is not true. I will tell you a story. Two repairmen were walking on the beach. They came upon a stretch of stranded starfish as far as their eyes could see. The first repairman picked up a starfish and threw it back in the sea. The second repairman scoffed. How could one repairman make a difference to so great a group of starfish? The first repairman picked up another starfish, threw it back in the ocean and said, 'well, I made a difference to that starfish.'"

"Dar why are you telling me that old story?"

"Because my friend, you make a difference to me. You are my friend."

Frank's cold heart began to warm around its edges.

"Dar, you old charmer. Linda never had a chance."

Thirty-three

THE WAITING ROOM

CHARLES TOLD EVELYN to meet him under the tree, by the dumpster shed, at two thirty in the afternoon. Evelyn had intended to meet him. She had intended to give him what he wanted, and to get out of his life. She looked down through the bare tree below her third floor window. Through its naked branches, she could see Charles waiting underneath the tree.

She stood back from the window in case he looked up and saw her. Her clock read one minute after four. When would he give up and believe she wasn't coming?

Evelyn had no idea where the diamond was. She had tried to buy time by saying she hid it at The Coffee Shop. He must know by now that it was not hidden there. By now, he might think she had left town with the diamond.

She sat on the floor by the window. Her studio reminded her of a cell. It was empty except for the pad she used for sleeping and the blue, tattered recliner which the last tenant had left behind. She got to her knees to peek out of the window. Charles was still waiting.

She went to her sleeping pad and laid down so she could consider the cracks in the ceiling. Their spidery lines always sparked her imagination. She smiled, and remembered the day she and Charles had stood outside the locked jewelry store. They could see Dar inside so they knocked hard and made pleading gestures at him.

Dar had seen their smiles and arms wrapped around each other. They were both a little wet from the light rain. Another couple in love needed his assistance. Though he had closed for the day, he unlocked the door and let them into his shop.

Evelyn pretended to be interested in this ring, then that ring, but she wanted the diamond that had been delivered that afternoon by a courier friend of Charles'. Dar had not yet deposited the diamond in his safe, and Charles could see the protective pouch, which contained the gem, behind the counter. Evelyn looked away when Charles threatened Dar, but looked adoringly at Charles when he gave the diamond to her on their way out.

"Why are you giving it to me?" she asked hoping for a proposal.

"I don't want to get caught with it, you fool. Listen carefully to me. You are worth something to me *if* you keep this safe. If anything happens to it, then something bad, something *really* bad, will happen to you."

Regret ran like acid rivulets through her brain. Why had she put the diamond in the dryer? It should have been safe there but who hides a diamond in a dryer anyway?

She sat up and banged her head on the wall, hoping to shake loose the self hatred that consumed her mind and devoured her hopes. Her waitress job was incinerated with the fire at the Coffee Shop. She had reached for love but grasped a phantom. She had no one, no money and soon, no home. "No … one … loves … you," she said to the beat her head made on the wall. "No … one … wants … you …"

She finally stopped pounding the wall when the pain in her head was stronger than the pain in her heart. It was four thirty. She crept to the window and looked down through the tree. Charles was gone.

Thirty-four

DETECTIVE LOU

THEY turned in early, so the father and son team got an early start the next day. In the truck, Frank asked Lou what Jay wanted to talk about.

Lou lied to protect his Dad's ego, "He said he'd be out of the apartment a lot and wanted us to have the keys."

"Oh? Well, where are they? I'll put them on my key ring," Frank said.

"Well, I guess since there's only one pair, I'll hold on to them, Dad."

Frank said nothing for the rest of the drive. He sensed his son was hiding something from him but he would appear insecure if he asked more questions. The phone was ringing when they entered the office. Frank took care of the call while Lou started coffee brewing.

"Clean and Cold Appliance ... Really? ... I'll call you back later." Frank hung up the phone.

"What did you do with that refrigerator on Delaware Street?" Frank asked Lou.

"Delaware? You said it was on Poplar," Lou said. From there the conversation took on a 'who's on first' quality.

"Poplar? I said it was on Delaware," Frank said.

172

"If you said it was on Delaware why did I go to Poplar?"

"Why would I say Poplar if the house was on Delaware? Look! Forget about it. You went to the wrong house. Get over to Delaware. Take the address this time, and take the delivery truck. And here's a few more calls for you." Frank handed Lou the accordion file and became absorbed in his computer screen.

Lou was embarrassed and sorry he had disappointed his Dad but he was excited to go on more service calls. He pulled out the work orders and studied them. Without taking his eyes from the computer Frank said, "Head over to the leaky dishwasher first. I've been out there already and I can't find anything wrong with it. Maybe you can get through to her. Plus, you won't have to backtrack like you did yesterday to hit the other calls."

Lou hung his head and walked out of the office. His dad had worked out yesterday's order of events. This time, Lou planned his route. He would check the smelly fridge after the dishwasher phantom leak because both addresses were in Melon Park. Then he would loop north to get the refrigerator from the correct address on Delaware. He grabbed the lunch bag he'd packed, checked his tools and drove south.

Lou rang the doorbell and heard a sucking noise from under the front door. When the large carved door swung open, he saw that the source of sucking sound was a Cocker Spaniel. Next to the pooch was an athletic looking woman who greeted him in black yoga pants and razor back tank top.

"Good morning, are you Lou? I'm Carol, please come in." She spoke quickly as if to rush him inside. On the way to the kitchen, she yelled up the stairway, "Kids, you'll be late for school! Come downstairs right now!" To Lou she said, "Come on, follow me. Every day it's the same thing. Here's the kitchen, I just need to pack these lunches. The leaky dishwasher is over there." She turned away from Lou and toward the bread and peanut butter on the counter. Lou saw the dishwasher but no leak.

"When's the last time you used the dishwasher, Carol?"

"Oh, I just unloaded it. I used it last night, but it didn't leak," she said licking grape jelly off a knife. It perplexed Lou that she had used the appliance without a leak. He wondered if she was pulling his leg. She continued, "It only leaks in the morning, about this time actually," she said.

"You mean it leaks spontaneously, even when you're not using it?" Lou asked.

"Yes that's right. Crazy, huh? Kyle! Caitlyn! Get down here right now!"

Galloping footsteps on the stairs heralded the children's arrival. They rushed into the kitchen and sat at the kitchen table. Immediately Carol filled their glasses and delivered breakfast plates.

Lou was on his own. He knelt down to take off the front panel of the dishwasher. The dark floor tile was cold but he lay down to get a look inside at the hoses. Evidently, the pooch was interested in the dishwasher too. The spaniel trotted over and lifted its hind leg. He aimed a stream of liquid at the washer, missing Lou by inches.

174

"Hey!" Lou shouted startling Carol, the kids and the cocker spaniel too. More gently he added, "M'am I think I've discovered the leak." Lou stood up and pointed to the puddle in front of the dishwasher.

"Did you know your dog relieved himself here in the morning?" he asked.

"Well, just imagine! I had no idea! I thought he held it 'til we went for our walk! I never dreamed it was Cookie. I was so busy taking care of the children, I didn't even notice. Well, how about that, I didn't need a repairman after all, my dishwasher doesn't leak," she said. Lou smiled, closed up the dishwasher and wrote out the bill.

"You're not charging me for this are you?" she asked incredulously. "You didn't do anything!"

Lou thought he *had* done something. For one thing, he saved himself and his Dad a trip to Carol's house again. He was sure his Dad had not charged her for the last time.

"Carol, I did expect to be paid for the time I spent here. After all, I discovered the problem. But if you feel strongly ..." Lou stopped when Carol's husband, Ken, walked into the kitchen.

"Hi, everybody happy?" he asked diplomatically. Carol reminded her husband about the morning dishwasher leaks, and then explained how the dog had lifted his leg while Lou was on the floor with his head in the dishwasher. When she got to the part about the dog relieving himself so close to Lou, Ken, Caitlin, Kyle, and finally Carol, laughed out loud.

"Well, Lou did the job we needed him to do. Our problem is solved if we remember to let Cookie out in the morning, so ... It seems fair we should pay the man.

175

What do you think, Carol?" Ken asked. Carol agreed, still in a good mood from telling an amusing story. Lou left the house paid, satisfied, and thankfully dry.

Lou hoped the next call was fast too. The owners, a wealthy retired couple, lived in a large home on a tree-lined street. Lou admired the large southern plantation type home, and thought his mother would have loved the abundant foliage bursting with petite white roses around the stately porch.

Both Mr. and Mrs. Arnold met Lou at the door and walked him passed a gallery of photos covering every inch of the hallway. Lou recognized local and national dignitaries with the Arnolds in the frames.

Finely loomed rugs covered the floors. Lou hoped his shoes were clean as they padded toward the kitchen. He checked his hands for dirt between glimpses of attractive furnishings and gilded frames around colorful paintings. In the bright and airy kitchen, expensive appliances and cabinets were housed under shiny granite countertops.

"We've never had a problem like this before. We keep our home impeccably cleaned. We've asked Juanita, our housekeeper, to clean the refrigerator many times but the smell never completely goes away," Mrs. Arnold said.

"In fact it comes and goes no matter what we do," Mr. Arnold added.

"I can't entertain until this is resolved," Mrs. Arnold added, punctuating the seriousness of the situation. In the kitchen, Lou noticed exposed framing where the kitchen wall should have been and asked, "Doing a remodel?"

"This is how bad it's gotten, Lou. We thought the smell might be coming from behind the walls so we tore through the drywall. It smelled fine in there though. I don't know why we thought our wall spaces would smell," he said glancing at his wife.

For some reason, Lou's mind flashed back to the time he left his Dad's old convertible top down in the rain. The story was too long to hold the attention of Mr. and Mrs. Arnold, but he remembered that the only time he smelled the bad mildew odor (his dad was not happy about that) that had developed in the car, was when the heater was on.

The couple smiled politely while Lou checked the refrigerator. He removed the panel to expose the compressor, fan and defrost pan. They all gasped. A stiff, long toothed rat lay lifeless in the pan.

"Oh! Well! I wonder where that came from ... Well, a rat, in *our* home ..." The couple stammered and blushed.

Lou explained that every time the fan came on, the smell of decaying rat was dispersed into the kitchen. The couple looked less than interested. So, Lou used an old sandwich bag he happened to have in his pocket to pick up the rat.

"I don't think you'll have the bad smell anymore," he said holding the bag out to the couple.

"Fine, just take it with you, will you?" Mr. Arnold asked.

"Well, actually, I don't have anywhere to put your rat in my truck," Lou said.

"Well, we're not keeping that here, you take him with you," Mrs. Arnold insisted. Rather than offend a customer, Lou added a small disposal fee to the bill and left with the recently deceased.

On the long drive north he unhitched his thoughts and daydreamed about Julia. He remembered how the morning light in the convent laundry room had sparked brilliant highlights in her hair. The memory was intoxicating. His heart felt full of something new, something unexpected. Like his jack-in-the-box had taught him when he was a child, if one kept cranking, something would change.

Thirty-five

FALLING

LOU avoided Poplar Avenue in case the towel-woman was outside and recognized him. When he found the correct house on Delaware, the house and the refrigerator were empty. Luckily, there was only one step out of the house because the load was unwieldy. He had sweat through his clean shirt by the time he got the fridge in the truck, and tied it down.

It felt good to finally be in the truck and on his way back to the shop. He had remembered to bring his lunch: delicious leftovers from a kind neighbor's delivery of roast beef au jus on two big French rolls with onions and gravy. He had forgotten to pack napkins, however, and some of the juice dribbled unnoticed onto the front of his work shirt.

He finished the last of the sandwich, and arrived at the shop in time to hear the office phone ringing. His Dad was nowhere in sight so he wiped his mouth on his sleeve, and answered the phone.

"Clean and Cold Appliance, how can I help you?"

"Hi, I need you to come over right away. I've got so much ice in my freezer I can't close the door," a woman's thin voice said quietly.

"Sounds like the freezer is over icing. I can help you with that but it would be better if you defrosted the freezer yourself before I came over. Just leave the door open and let the ice melt on its own. Empty the pan when it gets full of water. You don't want to pay me to stand there with a hair dryer defrosting your freezer before I can work on it," Lou said.

They both laughed and agreed she would call back to schedule an appointment when the freezer was defrosted.

Lou wondered where his Dad was. He got up from the desk to look for him in the showroom but before he could get around the desk the back door opened. A very large man, whose figure blocked the light from outside, stood in the doorway. When he stepped inside, another smaller man was revealed behind him.

"Hello, how can I help you today?" Lou asked professionally.

"I know what kind of refrigerator I want. The guy I talked to earlier said you had it in stock," the smaller man replied.

"Sure, follow me up front," Lou said. He helped them find the black refrigerator they wanted. Lou tried but could not find a foothold for small talk so he silently took them to the register and gave them a receipt for a cash purchase.

"I'll get the dolly for you…"

"Don't bother, we'll take care of it ourselves," the smaller man stated. Together, the quiet men rolled the refrigerator out of the shop. When Lou tried to help load their truck they refused assistance again.

"OK guys, well, thank you for your business. Goodbye!" Lou watched the men pull out of the lot with the refrigerator on the back of their pick-up truck. Sometimes people wanted what they wanted and they did not need anything from anyone. Lou thought his Dad sometimes acted this way. Frank's ears could have been burning because he pulled into the lot at that moment.

"Where you been?" Lou asked his Dad when he finally came into the office.

"The Convent called. One of the ovens in the kitchen wasn't working. I know they like their meals on time so I got up there right away. Hey, do you know Julia McAuley? She works up there with the retired Sisters."

Lou casually admitted knowing her. He wanted to know if Julia had feelings for him before he would say more.

"Yeah, the Sisters said you knew each other. She's up at Pills hospital with a broken hip," Frank stated.

Lou took the news like a punch to the stomach. Was she OK? Was she in pain? He had to see for himself. "When did this happen? I was just there yesterday!"

"I guess it was after you left. She was helping a Sister down the stairs. When the old girl lost her balance, Julia pushed her against the banister to save her, but Julia took the fall herself. She'll be in the hospital for a few days. Oh, here, an old buddy of mine called this morning. He's going on a fishing trip, but he wants you to stop by and fix the coils on his stove while he's gone. He'll leave the door open for you," Frank said, handing Lou the accordion file.

Lou cringed. Another "buddy" was leaving the house empty for him? He was about to ask his Dad if he could wait until the owner came home when the back door opened. There stood a familiar large man and his little buddy behind him.

"Hi, how can we help you?" Frank asked.

"I want my money back," the taller of the two said.

"Dad, these were the customers you talked to on the phone about the black Whirlpool Refrigerator. I sold it to them while you were at the Convent," Lou explained.

"Oh, yes, I remember our phone conversation, is there something wrong with the refrigerator, Sir?" Frank asked.

"Yes, you could say that. It fell off my truck and it looks like hell," the larger man stated dryly. Frank shot a woeful glance at his son.

"Which tie downs did you use, Son?" he asked. When Lou explained the men would not let him load the refrigerator, Frank said,

"I'll take care of this, Lou. Get up to San Gilberto and fix that stove."

Given the choice between dealing with these customers and dealing with an empty house, Lou was not sure which end of the stick he was getting. But he was sure he wanted to visit Julia in the hospital so he left quickly.

Out in the lot, he realized he had not unloaded the refrigerator from Delaware Street from the delivery truck. He decided to take the service truck instead.

To be responsible, he should go to San Gilberto first. But he took El Camino Boulevard so he could drive passed Pills Hospital on his way north. It pained him to think of Julia cooped up in a hospital room. She was energetic and smart so staying in bed would be frustrating for her. He reminded himself he did not really know Julia so how would he know how she felt? For all he knew she liked letting other people take care of her for a change. He put Julia out of his mind and focused on finding the address on Capuchin Avenue.

He parked the truck in front of an attractive, two story, Craftsman styled home and went up the steps to the large porch. He double checked that he had the correct address. The wooden planks that wrapped around the house creaked under his work boots. He reached for the door knob. It would not turn for him. He closed his eyes, leaned forward, and banged his head on the locked door. Behind closed eyes Lou wondered how well his Dad knew this old buddy. Well enough to know he was a little forgetful?

Irritated, Lou took a quick look around the property. He wanted to finish this repair so he could see Julia. Neither the French door on the side of the house nor the back door to the kitchen, were unlocked. Short of breaking in, he could not gain access to the house. So, he left his business card in the front window and ran to the truck.

Traffic on El Camino was light so he cruised along at a good speed. He hoped the spinning and flashing red lights which had suddenly lit up in his rearview mirror had nothing to do with him. He was approaching the hospital and if this was a traffic stop, he

would have to pull over right under the patients'
windows.

"Service truck, please pull over," the officer said
over the patrol car's loudspeaker. Unable to deny his
fate Lou pulled over across the street from the hospital.
He imagined every patient, in every window, and their
nurses and doctors beside them, watching the officer
cautiously approach Lou's truck.

"Sir, do you know why I pulled you over?"

"Um, well, I'm sorry if I was speeding, Sir. I
wasn't paying attention to my speed, I guess."

"Sir, your plate showed up in my system. Have
you been doing any work in San Gilberto?"

"Yes. Well, I mean no, but I tried. The house was
supposed to be open, but it wasn't, so I left my card."

"A neighbor called to report suspicious activity
on a property he knew to be vacant." The officer paused
and looked over the truck. Lou hoped if he said nothing
it would keep the exchange brief.

"License, Registration and Proof of Insurance,
please. You can be reached at the number on your
truck?"

"Yes, Sir, that's current." Frank had organized
the vehicle documents in a plastic storage bag. Lou
grabbed it from the glove compartment and handed it to
the officer.

"Here, keep the bag. OK, stay in your truck. I'll
be right back."

While waiting for the officer to return, Lou felt
most comfortable either looking straight ahead or into
his rearview mirror but not at the hospital. He was afraid
Julia, though stuck in her hospital bed with a broken hip,

184

would see him and assume he was in trouble with the law.

After an interminable wait, the officer returned. "OK, we'll leave it up to the home owner's discretion whether to pursue the investigation; I'm willing to let this go for now. Have a good day, Sir."

Lou's beating heart needed a break. The officer walked briskly to his patrol car. Lou wiped his wet palms on his trousers and took deep breaths until the rumba rhythm in his chest slowed to a cha cha. The cop was still parked behind him when Lou cautiously pulled out into traffic and into the left turn lane for the hospital parking lot.

"Excuse me, can you tell me what room Julia McAuley is in?" Lou asked the lady behind the information desk. Her gray hair was pulled back in a pony tail and yellow horses pranced over her royal blue hospital apron.

"Sure, honey. She's in 606. Just take that elevator behind you to the sixth floor. Take a right out of the elevator, go through the double doors. Once you're in the pink hallway, go left down hallway B06. Her room will be on the west side of the nurse's station."

Lou thanked her and rehearsed her instructions on the way to the elevator. Had she said the west side of the nursing station? He would need a compass to find Julia but if she was in this hospital, he would find her.

Once on the sixth floor, he asked each nurse, doctor and aide he passed for directions to room 606. He thought his heartbeat would have calmed by the time he found Julia's room but it beat faster the closer he got to it.

He paused at her door, planning his suave entrance. Should he rest his hand on the door and compliment her on the view? Or, should he knock and wait until she asked him in? Finally, he put on his most confident smile and marched into Julia's room.

When his eyes met Sister Martha's steady gaze, his suavity melted like ice in a hot pan. He had not expected Sister Martha to be in Julia's room and she seemed quite taken aback by him too. She put her hand on the large cross hanging from her neck and stared with fascination at his chest.

At first, Lou was surprised Sisters had attractions like this, but then he caught a glimpse of the shirt cuff he had used to wipe the sandwich remnants from his face. He looked down at the dark, au jus stains that dotted the front of his shirt. He also considered the aroma he might be emitting created by the exertion of moving the Delaware refrigerator, and by the nerves of the traffic stop. He looked to Julia with apprehension but she lay in bed with her eyes closed. She looked so pretty he nearly propelled himself to her bedside, but Sister's raised eyebrow and protective stance discouraged him from doing so.

"Hi ... Lou, right?" Sister asked.

"Oh, yes, hi Sister Martha, yes, it's Lou. Is Julia OK?"

"She'll be fine, her surgery went well, but the medicine she's taking for pain makes her sleepy. The good news is she'll be out of the hospital and back on her feet in a few days."

Julia's eyes opened and focused on Lou.

"Lou, I didn't expect to see you," she breathed, "Does the hospital need a repair?"

186

Lou smiled and stepped closer, holding her eyes with his so they would not fall on his shirt.

"No Julia, I'm not here to repair anything. I'm here to see you. But I am a little jealous of the doctor that got to fix you. Are you OK?"

"Sure, I'm fine. My hips were too big anyway. I asked the surgeon to make me pear shaped instead of watermelon."

Lou smiled and asked, "Did you fall down a lot of steps?"

"I don't know. I didn't count them on the way down," she teased drowsily.

"Well, you'd better get back on your feet; I hear they need you to fix some appliances at the Convent."

"Believe me, there's nothing I want more than to get back on my feet. It's making me crazy cooped up in here. Maybe you can bring me a cake with a file in it ..."

Sister Martha interrupted, "Julia you need to rest, but you'll be out soon. It's hard to keep a good woman down."

"Then Julia will be up and around fast, right Sister? Julia? I'll be in the neighborhood tomorrow. I thought maybe I could stop by and visit you again?"

Julia smiled and nodded affirmatively, but her heavy eyelids closed before she could say yes.

"Well, I'll leave you to rest. I just wanted to see you, Julia. I was so sorry to hear you got hurt, and, well, I'll see you tomorrow."

Julia's eyes were still closed but she smiled and said, "Drive carefully, Lou. The police are everywhere." Sister Martha chortled. "Thanks for coming to visit, Lou. You're a good friend. Don't worry, she'll be fine."

So they did witness him talking to the police! Lou touched his hot cheeks with his moist palms. On his way to the sixth floor elevator, he tried to remember only the positive parts of the visit. It was a positive that Julia had not seemed to notice his shirt, or been upset that he had been talking to the police. Of course, that could have been because of the pain medication, but a positive was a positive. He was thrilled to see that she was OK, and that was good too.

She looked stunningly beautiful, and the best part was, she wanted him to visit tomorrow. So what if he was a little embarrassed? He promised himself that tomorrow, he would make an impressive impression on this beautiful girl.

Thirty-six

NOT THE PLAN

FOR THE FIRST TIME EVER, Frank woke his son for work. Lou had stayed up late doing laundry. Pressed work shirts and pants hung on every door ledge in Lou's room. They both ate and left for work. The shop was freezing when they arrived.

"You're sipping your coffee like a princess. What's with the bib?" Before Lou could answer, the phone rang and his Dad picked it up.

"M'am I know you're upset but I cannot understand what you're saying; would you please lower your voice for me?" Frank aimed a sharp look at Lou who braced himself against the chair.

"So what you're saying is, you left the hair dryer on high in your freezer, you forgot about it, and now the plastic liner of the freezer is melted? And someone from our shop told you to do this?"

Lou could not believe his ears. He did not tell the woman to leave a hairdryer in her freezer. Frank finished the call and spoke in a friendly, if slightly sarcastic, tone.

"Good news. We have a new customer. She'll be down a little later. She needs a new refrigerator, at a discount of course ..."

"Dad, she called earlier and told me her icebox had frozen over. I told her she didn't want to pay me to stand there with a hair dryer. Man, what is going on with me? Am I bad luck?" Lou asked holding his head in his hands. Frank rarely witnessed anything but a "cup half full" attitude from Lou and given his strange behavior lately, Frank intervened.

"You're just tired from staying up, Lou. Don't worry about the hairdryer lady. We'll work it out."

Frank's kindness weakened an emotional dike inside Lou. He was tired and he had not slept well from worrying about Julia. He lowered his face and let spill a litany of calls gone wrong. The Hillswood owner who left the security alarm on, the police in front of the hospital, the towel lady, the terrier, (even though his Dad already knew about that), the refrigerator that fell off the truck (even though he didn't have anything to do with that) and last but not least, a melted freezer.

"Lou, come on, what about all of the great things you've done? You solved the mystery of the mysterious dishwasher leak, and the mystery of the mysterious disappearing soap powder, and you even convinced Mrs. Faxon that her washer spin cycle worked. If this repair thing doesn't work out you can try detective work!"

"What do you mean? You don't think this repair thing is working out?" Lou asked.

"No, No, Lou, listen. I know it's tough, but you've got to pay your dues like anyone else. Hey, it wasn't always easy for me in the beginning either, you know. One time a customer came down here after I had worked at his ex-wife's house. He demanded the alimony money he said I stole off her kitchen table. Threatened to call the police on me if I didn't give it

190

back. I didn't take his damn money and I sweat bullets for months thinking the police were going to take me away! One day out of the blue, the guy's ex wife called me to come over to her house again. She wanted me to clear out her washing machine. Can you believe I had to teach the lady to clean her cloth diapers before she washed them? Anyway, when I was done I asked her about the alimony money her husband said I stole. She just laughed and said her kids had hidden the money from her but they found it months ago." Frank shook his head. "And don't worry about the police. I've worked in this County for a long time. The cops know we're alright, but they have to do their job too. It's just part of what we have to deal with, OK son?" Lou felt better and asked about the guys whose refrigerator fell off their truck.

"Don't worry about them. Turns out I knew the tall guy's Dad. We served together in the war. I gave them a deal on the fridge you left in the truck from Delaware Street. OK, now you're all better. Why don't you take a hike out to Franklin Valley? Mother Nature called." Frank handed Lou two service orders.

"And to show you how much confidence I have in you, I'm sending you to fix our old friend Janet's refrigerator. Don't screw this one up, Lou." Lou appreciated the confidence but was the threat necessary? He would focus on his plan to visit Julia after the job.

The ride to Franklin Valley was beautiful and it calmed Lou's nerves. He cruised carefree through the shade of tall pines, cedars and an occasional shaft of dusty sunlight. He had been to the Valley Ranch many times with his Dad so he knew how to find the shrub framed driveway.

Janet waved to him from the door of the old barn. She lived by herself on the property, unless you included all of her animals. Her salt and pepper hair was pulled back into a pony tail and her blue jean and plaid shirt style had not changed in the years Lou had known her. She was a regular customer, and Frank and Lou learned what a good friend she was when she came to Mae's funeral.

"Hey Lou! Glad we got some sunshine today. Not so cold, eh? How are you? How's your Dad doing? I've got a problem here let me tell you!" Janet never paused for an answer so Lou listened patiently.

"Lou, the problem is rats. I don't have a problem with them personally but they're eating my chicken feed. So, I figured I'd better get some cats to kill these rats. I got two cats from the animal shelter. I don't know where they are now. Ricky? Lucy? They're shy. Anyways, now I've got more mouths to feed, right? No problem, these trees are full of nests in the spring and the kitties love the little birdies! I keep the dead birds for the cats in the fridge or they'll go bad during the year, you know. But, like I told your dad, the fridge ain't workin'."

Lou imagined Janet up in the trees searching nests for her cat food. He was not in the city anymore. He grabbed his tools and a tarp.

The pair walked into the barn where sunlight streamed through old plank walls, and shed light on the straw covered floor.

"So, the cats swallow the birds to catch the rats that eat the feed?" he asked enjoying the memory of his Mom's favorite rhyme. A wave of grief overwhelmed him at the thought of her.

"Well, not if I don't get this fridge fixed!" She laughed and her amusement released Lou from his memories of his mom. He spread a tarp on the ground behind the refrigerator and knelt to investigate.

"Janet, I'm afraid there's been some foul play here. It looks like those dirty rats sabotaged the fridge. They built nests in the base of the refrigerator. The nests clogged up the fan. You'll have a cold refrigerator once I clean it out. That should reestablish the food chain."

Lou removed the fan, cleaned it out, and got the fridge temperature going in the right direction. Janet was relieved when the job was done and it occurred to her she had another problem.

"Lou, would you have a look at the old clothes washer in the back here? It fills up but it won't drain," she explained.

Lou avoided looking at his watch and answered, "Sure, Jan." Julia would still be in the hospital when he got there, but Janet needed his help now. He checked the hose outlets, daintily keeping his knees from the ground, and asked, "Janet, what have you been washing in here?"

"Big, fat walnuts," she answered.

"Big, fat walnuts?"

"Oh, it's fantastic. You see, the walnuts come off the tree with a kind of green skin around the shells. I came up with an amazing idea. I wash off the tough skins from the walnuts in the washing machine. So, all I'm left with is a clean walnut. I shell the walnuts later, at my convenience."

While Lou dug out the skins from the pump, he patiently explained the connection between the washer's

193

clogged drain hose and Janet's amazing idea. Finally, they settled the bill.

"Well, you've just about solved all my problems today, Lou. Thanks a lot. Be sure and say hello to your Dad."

"Will do, Janet. Just call if you need us," Lou said sincerely. Janet watched and waved to Lou until he was off the property.

The unusually balmy winter weather ushered in a wave Lou's confidence. He felt pretty good about being able to solve people's problems. And with customers like Janet, who found such creative uses for their appliances, he knew he would always have a job.

While his uniform was still clean and his confidence was still high, Lou made his way to visit Julia in the hospital. He had visited her the day before empty handed. Determined to be everything he was not yesterday, he decided to buy her something impressive at the hospital gift shop.

The giant, oversized stuffed bear for sale was almost twice his own girth but probably too cute for Julia's sophisticated tastes. Lou thought she would prefer flowers, but the scant bud vase selection was unimpressive. Luckily, in a corner of the store he had overlooked, he discovered a large flower arrangement similar in size to the bear.

He walked out of the gift shop carrying the heavy vase. Luckily, he knew his way to the elevator because it was hard to see through the arrangement. He met other visitors waiting for the elevator but ignored their astounded stares. It seemed to Lou, they acted as if it was the first time they had seen a flower bouquet.

The elevator arrived and Lou got in first. "Would you please push six for me?" Lou asked from behind the vase.

As the doors opened on ascending floors, more people got on than got off, so Lou was pushed to the back corner of the elevator. He kept the flowers elevated above his shoulders so as not to bruise the blossoms.

Finally, the elevator arrived at the sixth floor.

"Excuse me, sorry, excuse me" Lou said to the successive rows of fellow elevator riders. He lost a few buds on the low doorway of the elevator but to Lou's relief, most of the flowers looked OK. He discovered if he held the vase on his hip, he could see the hallway in front of him.

He reached Julia's room. He stopped for a moment to check his shirt for spots and to take a deep breath. He peered around the flowers into Julia's room which, he was relieved to see, was empty except for Julia. Her eyes were closed and he savored her beautiful face for a moment.

"Julia?"

She opened her eyes and smiled at Lou, and the bountiful blooms.

"How are you feeling?" Lou asked stepping into the room.

Julia was not sure how she should answer Lou's question. "Trapped" in the hospital, she had had a lot of time to think. The ordeal she had endured comprised of falling, fracturing her hip, surgery, and now recuperation. It trapped the energy inside her like champagne in a corked bottle. The minute she was released she would seize the day. Her life had been tossed in the air and it was time to plan the landing so she could hit the ground running. But in which direction should she run? And how did this man standing before her, dwarfed by a ridiculously sized bouquet, fit into her plan?

"Come in, sit down. I'm glad you're here, I've been thinking about you. We need to talk."

Lou tried to put the vase on Julia's nightstand but he nearly knocked over a pitcher of water. He caught the pitcher with one hand but his other hand slipped on the vase. He had just enough time to grab the mouth of the vase before it hit the floor.

The windowsill was large and empty so he carefully placed the bouquet in front of the window. He looked for a chair and found one at the foot of Julia's bed. He tried to pull the chair around the bed but he backed it into Julia's bed table, which was hovering over her bed. Apologetic, he carefully wheeled the bed table away from her and put it against the wall so he could move his chair close to her. Finally, he sat down.

Julia took a deep breath. She had spent a restless night listening to the beeps, calls, and general bustle of hospital nightlife. The same question that agonized her nights burned in the daylight. Should she confide her dilemma, or wait until she made her decision? Having Lou by her side made her feel alive and happy but it did not give her clarity.

"I'm doing really well, Lou. The surgery went better than the doctors expected and I've already been on my feet. I'm doing laps around the nurse's station; all I need is a race number. They say I can go home tomorrow."

"Well, you look great. I'm glad you're doing so well too."

"Um, thanks for those flowers, Lou. They're very … impressive." She was silent, but instinctively Lou knew there was more she wanted to say.

"Lou, I know we've just gotten to be friends, but I feel close to you. That's why it's important to tell you about something I've been wrestling with."

"Sure, Julia, I want to know everything you're thinking."

"I am thinking of taking vows."

Lou's stomach sucked in and turned over. He had toyed with the idea of kissing her but the 'Convent' word cooled his jets. Suddenly, the flowers seemed ridiculous and he felt like a fool.

"Julia, I'm sorry, I didn't mean to … it's just that I thought … you're like no one I've ever met …" he blurted before he could stop himself. With nothing to lose, he threw caution to the wind.

"Julia, wait. Do you think we could get to know each other a little better before you decide? I won't stop you from doing anything you want. I just think we should take a little time …"

"Lou, I haven't decided for sure but, I've been thinking about this long before I met you. I've talked to Mother Superior and she says I can start my preparation when I'm healed. I like you very much Lou, I just don't want to …" she stopped not wanting to finish.

"You don't want to lead me on. I understand. But, we can still see each other, right?" He finished his plea and Sister Martha entered the room.

"Lou, how nice of you to visit Julia. And my! What an enormous arrangement!" she exclaimed walking over to the window. "Sister Therese will want to study this one. She does the flower arranging at the

Convent and she loves to deconstruct the bouquets we receive," Sister Martha said.

The enormity of Julia's intentions was catching up with Lou and he did not care what happened to the flowers, he just needed to escape quickly.

"I should be going; my dad needs me. I'm glad to see how well you're doing, Julia. 'Bye Sister Martha. Oh, Sister Therese is welcome to the flowers," Lou said on his way out.

Julia wanted to stop him and say something consoling but she said nothing. She had nothing consoling to offer. Lou stopped at the door. He had the feeling he had forgotten something. Julia hoped he would turn around and say something to fix all of the turmoil in her heart. Instead, he continued out of the room.

Thirty-seven

THE END

BIG SCREEN TVs were prohibited in Jay's apartment building. He thought people living in affordable housing, such as he provided, should own simple appliances. Despite this policy, Jay heard loud voices coming from an upstairs apartment. He had not noticed any TV deliveries, but his tenants could be sneaky.

He strode righteously up the stairs, following the voices. His pace slowed as he neared the door of the offending apartment. A crazed man peppered his rant with curses, and a woman cried through her pleas. This reality show was not on the television.

Conflict resolution was not in Jay's job description so he turned to go. It took one word to cause his retreat to a halt, "... diamond ..." His curiosity peaked, he pressed his ear to the door.

"What do you mean you put the damn diamond in a dryer you fool ass girl? I know you have it! Give it to me NOW 'fore I blow your head off!"

"Please, please, I swear ... Owww ... Owww! Stop! I don't have, owww! They took it! I swear, the same people who took your Mama's old refrigerator took the dryer. They took it! Please!" Evelyn whimpered and pleaded but her weakness enraged him.

Jay smiled. He had wondered about this woman's past and if she had secret means to pay her rent. He had not guessed she was involved in the jewelry store robbery up the street. That diamond was worth more money than his little brother would ever make, or dream of making. What if she *had* hidden the diamond in the dryer that Exelda and Lamar removed? Jay reasoned that if he could keep it from the cops, legally it was his dryer so it was *his* diamond.

Suddenly, a loud blast reverberated from behind the door. Jay ran for the stairwell. He leapt down the stairs, two at a time, and reached the next landing when he heard the ominous sound of fast moving footsteps in the stairwell above him. Jay scurried behind the second floor door where he waited, his heart pounding. He closed his eyes and willed the fleeing footsteps to pass him and continue out of the building.

The danger had passed. He wiped his brow and looked back up the stairwell. He breathed heavily and climbed the stairs toward the thief's apartment. In an effort to avoid being shot himself, he whistled to announce his approach. The door was slightly ajar, but Jay knocked forcefully. The door swung open.

Though the sight of the gaping wound in Evelyn's head was nauseating, it was a relief to know she could not shoot him. Jay was sorry for her loss, but his gain mattered more. He closed and locked the door with his key, then retreated to his apartment where he would plan his retirement.

Thirty-eight

COLD

LOU tossed and turned all night. When he slept, he dreamed of burning wildflower fields and suffocating avalanches of dirty laundry. The rest of the night, he stared at the darkness from the inside of his eyelids and counted the number of times he made a fool of himself in front of Julia.

An hour before his alarm would go off he gave up and got up. He was not hungry but he threw a few snacks and a couple of sandwiches in a bag and left the house. Frank had given him two service calls yesterday evening. The first, not surprisingly, at a vacant home. The morning was cold and drizzly which Lou blamed for his uncharacteristic blues.

He was on his way to Franklin Valley again. He refrained from informing his Dad of the bad planning. His Dad should have tagged this trip onto yesterday's trip to Janet's animal feed and nut farm, which was also in Franklin Valley. Even worse, the house's owner was on a hunting trip but promised to leave the key under the doormat.

Lou drove the same route as yesterday, but it was difficult to recognize today. The tree lined road was dark, foggy and wet. Yesterday he had had the windows

201

rolled down and the radio turned up. Today he needed the wipers, defroster, heater and headlights.

Thanks to a reflector-decorated mailbox, he found the parking pad on the street below his Dad's friend's cabin. He got out of the truck and peered up through the mist to a cabin perched precariously on a fern covered mountainside.

Lou was tired and sore from not sleeping and his toolbox felt heavier than usual. He sighed at the foot of a long staircase, which climbed the steep grade to the cabin's porch.

By the time he reached the top of the stairs the chill had crept passed his burning thighs and into his bones. He wished he had grabbed a coat from home. He reached for the key under the doormat. There was no key. His breath steamed up the air around him. His hands ached with cold.

For the first time since his Dad had hired him, Lou felt angry. He resolved to complete his mission. He left his heavy toolbox by the front door and hunted for an open window. He found one, about six feet off the hill. He hoisted one leg at a time through the window and into the cabin. Once inside, he hung on the windowsill from his elbows and slowly lowered his body, hoping the floor was near. One of his feet touched down on something, but it slipped and he felt a wet sensation in his sock. He looked over his shoulder and saw the toilet bowl in which he had found a foothold.

Cursing he stepped out of the water and onto the floor. Responsibly, he locked the window he had come through to prevent a legitimate break-in. He squished through the house, which felt colder than outside, and retrieved his tools from the front porch. At least, he told himself, only one foot was wet and the toilet had been flushed.

The cabin was small but he noticed a little tinsel covered Christmas tree by a cold wood stove. Another holiday he and his dad would spend alone. Finally, he found the laundry room and the vintage Westinghouse washer. Any other time, Lou would have appreciated the unique glass front door of the washer, but cold and disappointment dulled his passion. He wanted to fix it and get back to his warm truck.

He turned on the washer to check the water level. Hot water churned in the round window. He knelt down in front of the machine. He balanced with one hand on the glass door, and he opened his tool box with the other hand. Suddenly, he heard a crackle. He turned in time to see the hot glass window splinter like a web around his freezing cold hand.

On another day, he might have laughed at the odds of such an accident. Today (with a cold soaking foot, little sleep and aching heart) Lou cursed. Despite his efforts to complete the job, including forced entry, he could not complete it. Special parts would be needed to repair the door. Defeated, he left an apology note and carefully made his way down the slippery, hillside staircase.

⧖

Back at the shop, Frank was on the phone with Jay Bicho.

"You're going to sell them and make money off them! I know the law Frank and you broke it. I want the machines back."

"Jay, you asked us to haul away those appliances. I don't understand what has changed, we have the same arrangement with all old appliances. Those machines aren't worth any money and I told you I don't make any money off the haul."

"Fine, keep the refrigerator if it's so important to you, just give me the dryer back."

"I can't give it back, Jay. The dryer's motor was out so I scrapped it."

"That's not good enough, Frank. I want the dryer back, or else. If you can't do it, I'll go to Exelda myself. Damnit, I'll sue if I have to, do you hear me?! And tell Lou to get over here. I've got a problem in 309." Jay hung up abruptly.

Frank was shaken. He had had a good business relationship with the Bichos until then. What had gone wrong? He wondered if Jay's strange behavior had anything to do with Lou and their cozy new relationship.

Frank valued the Bichos as customers, but he would remain loyal to his business partnership with Exelda and Lamar. The appliances they had taken from Jay's apartment now belonged to them. Jay would have to get in line or cut away. He looked up at the sound of the back door opening.

"Hi, Pop," Lou said. He sat in the chair in front of his Dad's desk.

"Why are you taking your shoes off in here?" his Dad asked.

"I've got some bad news about the Franklin Valley cabin," Lou said pulling off the wet sock. Without a replacement sock, he would wear his shoe sockless.

"Lou, Jay just called. He wants those machines Exelda hauled away last week."

"He does? What does he want those junkers for?" Lou asked.

"He says he's going to sell them for scrap. I'm not taking any business away from Exelda just so Jay can start a new hobby. Just to warn you, our love affair with the Bichos might be coming to an end. We're not choosing them over Lamar and Exelda. We will remain loyal even if the Bichos don't." He looked at Lou hoping for agreement. Lou, however, was focused on his shoes. He did not like the feel of the leather against his bare feet. Frank did not like his son's silence.

"Before you go to Melon park, Jay wants you at the apartments. Says he has a problem in 309 you need to fix. Oh, and don't forget you need to get to Melon Park," Frank said, glaring suspiciously at Lou and handing him the accordion file.

It felt funny wearing just one sock, even if it was dry. He took off his other shoe and the one dry sock, wrapped the wet sock in the dry one and put them both into his toolbox. When he had both shoes on, he considered his Dad's perspective.

His feelings about Jay had changed since he had gotten the keys to the apartment. Jay must have a good reason for wanting the dryer, and his dad could be unreasonable. Maybe he could help smooth things over between them. He ignored his Dad's glare, got in the truck and drove to Main Street.

The loading space was open in front of the Bicho building so he parked there and got out. He crossed paths with a utility gas man, also headed for the apartment.

"Hey, you know anything about the meter for this place?" he asked.

"No, sir, I'm an appliance man. I don't touch the meters."

"Well, somebody's been stopping the counter on their meter. They took off the glass head and jammed it. I'm going to have to lock these things up. People are no damn good these days," he said scornfully.

"They haven't surprised me yet. Hey, let me let you in the building so you don't have to wait for the buzzer." Lou conspicuously pulled the master key from his new retractable belt key holder and purposefully opened the front door of the apartment. Feeling like the king of the castle with the keys to prove it, he scaled the first two flights of stairs with one burst of energy. The last flight he climbed slowly, one step at a time. He paused at the door of 309 until he caught his breath, then knocked loudly on the door. There was no answer. He knocked again.

Jay had given him permission to use the key, so he unlocked the door and stepped inside.

"Appliance man!" His voiced echoed through the small apartment. He took his key out of the lock. He closed the apartment door, and while scouting for bugs, stepped gingerly across the room. He had no work order but there were only a few appliances in the kitchen to check. Then, something caught his eye.

"Oh, hello," he said to a woman wearing a black track suit, and reclining in the single piece of furniture in the apartment. She stared at the ceiling. He took a step forward before he reconsidered his approach.

The fabric behind the woman's head was glistening in crimson and gray. He followed the straight line of her limp arm to the floor where a forbidding, black pistol lay. Lou's thoughts were jumbled like towels in a dryer. She did not need medical assistance because she was clearly dead. A broken appliance was the least of her problems.

Slowly, he stepped backwards keeping his eye on the pistol. The sound of his toolbox hitting the door behind him made him jump. He wanted to get out of there. He was almost out the door without locking it. He realized a dead woman would not care if her door was locked or unlocked. He locked it anyway, out of habit.

Lou flew down the stairs to inform Jay. Jay was heading out the front door when Lou got to the bottom of the stairs.

"Jay I have to talk to you about 309, I've got some bad news," Lou called.

"Lou, just fix it. I'm tired of dealing with that woman, and I'm late for class," Jay said without stopping.

"Jay, it's not that easy, you've got a problem."

"Lou, she's your problem now, I have to go," Jay said stepping into the street.

"Jay. The woman in 309 is dead."

Jay smirked, crossed the street and disappeared around the corner. Lou was stunned. He was stymied. Did Jay expect him to call the police? Frank had told Lou to trust the police but the police might want to have a long discussion with Lou about his discovery of a woman, freshly inflicted with a gun shot to the head.

There was no time for a discussion with police because he had an appointment to keep with new, very wealthy clients. Lou rationalized that the woman in 309 would be no less dead waiting for the police, but a potentially influential client would become impatient waiting for Lou. That solved, he drove to Melon Park.

Thirty-nine

IT'S HOW YOU LOOK AT IT

HE was a high-tech salesman and she was a computer engineer. The young couple purchased their home because it had an in-law cottage behind the main house. Though the previous tenants of the cottage were actual in-laws, the information power couple planned to use it to party and to watch sports on a big screen TV. Additionally it would be the perfect bunkhouse for overflow guests like their parents, if they visited from the east coast.

With pride of ownership, they gave Lou a tour of the newly remodeled bunkhouse, and showed off its expensive centerpiece staircase. They had replaced the old narrow steps and its motorized chair lift with a spiral, cherry wood staircase to match the newly installed cherry wood floors.

The bunkhouse was perfect for the couple except for one thing. There was an old refrigerator on the second floor. They realized they needed to remove it *after* they had replaced the staircase. Now there was no prudent way to get the huge appliance down the elegant steps.

The couple led Lou up the new staircase to the second floor where the massive refrigerator was ensconced.

"Lou, we just know you'll be able to solve this riddle for us because we've heard such wonderful things about you. What we were thinking is that you could take the refrigerator apart, and bring it down piece by piece. We have no need for it." The young wife spoke in a reasoned, monotone voice.

Lou took his pinky and brushed a stray lock of hair from his forehead. The staircase was narrow, and taking apart this refrigerator might not be the most practical or even realistic solution.

"When we were outside I noticed a crate of new windows in the backyard, are you planning to install them up here?" Lou asked.

"Yes, yes, we are. The window panes in here are so large our windows had to be custom made. They were very expensive. One thousand dollars for each window. The workmen parked the large debris box out there so we can just drop the old windows down into them. Why do you ask?" The husband smiled curiously. He loved a good riddle.

"It would take a lot of time and therefore expense to take apart the refrigerator and even then, I couldn't rule out the possibility of damaging the staircase when we removed the pieces."

"Well, of course we don't want to waste our money or your time and you are correct in assuming that the staircase is the priority," the engineer wife stated plainly.

"Well, you know, I think we could just roll the refrigerator to the window, push it out, and let it drop into your debris box out there. The window is big enough."

The couple opened their eyes wide at Lou then at each other. Finally the salesman said, "I'll get the video camera."

Lou secured the refrigerator doors and shimmied the refrigerator to the window. On the count of three, Lou and the engineer pushed the refrigerator out of the window, and into the dumpster below while the salesman filmed. The refrigerator landed on target and made a spectacular crash.

"Lou, you are absolutely amazing, who would have ever thought of doing that?! Well, *we* could have, but I guess we needed your fresh perspective!" the engineer gushed. Lou's cheeks flushed from the compliment and the exertion of pushing the refrigerator out of the window. His mind flashed to the poor dead woman for whom he had done nothing, and he felt ashamed. He would not have wanted the same for his mother when she died.

"You're welcome, and listen, I've got to go, but don't worry about the bill, I didn't do anything," he said walking out toward the truck.

"Oh, it was something all right, and we will certainly tell our friends about you!" the salesman called.

In the security of his truck Lou's emotions were in turmoil. Finally he was doing the work he wanted since he was a little boy, but he was not happy. What would it take for him to be satisfied?

The day flashed before his eyes like a slideshow. Get out of bed exhausted and cold. Drop land into a toilet bowl. Crack a washer window with icy hands.

Discover a woman with a bullet in her head. Impress a brilliant wealthy couple. Had he had anything to eat? Truly, this had been a horrible day, but it had not beat yesterday. That was the day he learned the woman he loved wanted to enter a Convent.

He drove in a discouraged haze back to the appliance shop and parked in the back lot. He turned off the ignition, and rested his head on the steering wheel. A knock on the passenger window shook him from his fog.

"Jay! What are you doing here? I thought you had a class to go to," Lou said startled.

Jay climbed into the truck. "Heck of a day, I need a drink, how about you, Lou?"

Lou drank on rare occasions. Suddenly, a drink in the middle of the day sounded like a great idea. He drove to a neighborhood bar around the corner from the shop.

Twinkling Christmas lights hung around the room provided the only light in the bar. A few patrons watched a football game on a big screen TV behind the bar. Jay bought a 50 ml bottle of Crown Royal and set two shot glasses across from one another at a private corner table. Jay filled Lou's glass, then his own.

"To new horizons!" Jay smiled and clinked Lou's glass. They both drank enthusiastically to new horizons.

"Jay, I don't know how to tell you this, but, there's a dead woman in 309. I don't know if she did it to herself, or someone else did, but it looks like a gun was involved," Lou whispered.

"Lou, I know all about 309. I knew about it before I sent you up there."

Lou started. He knew? Why had Jay sent him in there if he knew? Why was Jay so calm?

"Don't, *don't* disappointment me, Jay. I defended you."

"Against who? Your Dad? Like I need defending against him," Jay snorted.

"OK, Jay, now what? Did you kill that woman?" Lou asked.

"No, I can honestly say, I did not kill that woman. But you might have. That's what the police will think when they find out you were the last one in the apartment, and they'd be right. She's dead because your idiot father would not give me my dryer back. He assumed I wanted it back for myself. Wrong. I wanted it back to save a woman's life. Now it's too late. Too bad. That girl meant a lot to me," Jay said with a poker face. He took a sip of his whiskey. Lou drank an entire shot. Jay refilled Lou's glass to the brim.

"Why would the dryer save her life?" Lou said.

"Like you don't know."

"Jay, you're not making any sense. We always scrap your appliances. Why don't you quit playing games and tell me what the hell you're up to?" Lou liked how bold he felt so he emptied another shot of liquid courage into his empty belly. Jay refilled Lou's glass.

"Lou, let's say I believe you don't know anything about the 8 carat diamond hidden in my dryer. Exelda was the last one to touch the dryer, and you were the last one in apartment 309. When the police put all the pieces of the puzzle together, they're going to solve a diamond robbery and a murder. Good for them, bad for you."

Lou's mind was trying to keep up with the new facts but his brain was slow in responding. One minute

213

he was putting Jay in his place and the next he was under Jay's boot.

"Diamond? What diamond robbery? You mean Dar's diamond?" He took a slug of Crown. Jay refilled Lou's glass and continued.

"OK, look, it's not all that bad, Lou. Sure, you'll be framed for murder if you don't do as I say, but what if you do? This can be really easy, Lou! Just get the dryer back from Exelda, give it back to me and you are off the hook."

"Wait. There's a diamond in the dryer? Does Exelda know this?"

"Everyone knows this. The murderer knows too. Guess where he's going next to look for the diamond? At least I might be able to save one life, Exelda's, if you *get me that dryer*."

Lou wished his thoughts were forming as fast as the beads of sweat on his forehead.

"Lou, if you were working for me you wouldn't be in this mess now, would you? You should have left your Daddy's shabby shop when you had a chance. Get me the dryer. I won't tell the police you killed that girl, and you can be the big hero who saves Exelda's life."

Lou gulped down the shot in front of him and blinked. When he opened his eyes, he was in his truck in front of Julia McAuley's house. He smacked his dry mouth and rubbed his neck. His head ached and he was filled with dread it *wasn't* just a bad dream that had awakened him. How long had he been sleeping in front of the McAuley's house?

He ran his fingers through the waves of his short hair and retrieved Jay's offer from his foggy memory. Jay would tell the police that Lou killed the woman in apartment 309 if he did not get the dryer back from Exelda.

Anxiety threatened to overwhelm his whiskey sodden mind. So Dar's 8 carat diamond is in the dryer he ordered to be scrapped. Had Exelda found the diamond and not told his Dad? How could he suspect her after knowing her all his life? Would Jay really frame him for murder if he did not get the dryer back for him? How could he betray Dar by giving the stolen diamond to Jay? How did he get himself in the middle of all this?

He did not want to scare Julia with his problems but he needed to be with her and by now she should be out of the hospital and home. He got out of the truck and walked up to the house. The birds singing from the towering trees around the property seemed particularly loud. He rang the doorbell.

Forty

THE GARDEN

"LOU," Julia said opening the door, "what a nice surprise, come in." Her smile melted his tension. He left his anxiety on the doorstep and stepped into her home. He was not sure what he should say, or even why he was there, but it was an oasis amidst a wasteland of uncertainty.

Julia led him into the kitchen. "I feel like an invalid with this cane," she said. "Would you like a soda?" Julia opened a can of soda and filled a glass for Lou. By the time she had put the can in the recycle bin he had emptied his glass. Without asking, she refilled the glass with another soda.

"I see you're limping but I'm glad you're up and around, Julia. You had us all pretty worried."

"I have something to show you," she said. She took him out the back door, holding his arm down the patio steps. He cleared his head by filling his lungs with the cool air scented with fir and fireplaces. He craned his neck to the tops of the beautiful redwood trees in her backyard. They walked to the edge of the patio where he was startled to find a large aviary.

"This is what I wanted to show you."

"That's a lot of canaries you have there, Julia. They're cute," he said nosing up to the cage. The coop was a little taller than he was and, "as wide as my wingspan," he joked.

"My parents gave me a pair of canaries on my sixteenth birthday and my father built this for them. I've raised canaries every year since then. I keep the males and females separate, you see? There is a moveable partition between them. I know the time is approaching for them to mate when the males start feeding the females through the partition screen."

Lou looked at her quizzically, "Really? That seems so tender. Do they choose the same mates every year?"

"Yes, it really is sweet. Sometimes the males can't wait until I reunite them. One day I came home to find a male had tried to sneak through to the female side but had gotten stuck between the mesh. He must have been stuck in front of the girls for hours. It was too soon to mate so I got a hold of him and put him back with the males. He wasn't hurt but for some reason he wasn't popular with the females that year," she said with a wink. Lou appreciated the dedication it required to raise these birds for so many years. "My favorite part is when the babies are born," she said.

Lou was not sure how to have a conversation about canaries, but birds had always intrigued him. "I've always wondered how they learn to fly. Seems like if they try to fly before they're ready they don't live to make that mistake again."

"If they're startled they might fly before they're ready but I've never had a problem. They know when they're ready."

217

Lou caught a movement out of the corner of his eye and turned to see a cat on the fence. It stared with green eyes into the aviary and its tail moved back and forth like a fluffy whip.

"Hey, who's that?"

"That's my neighbors' cat, CeeCee."

"How come the birds aren't afraid of the cat?" Lou asked.

"Dunno, but they're not. She loves watching the birds, it's her entertainment. The only thing I've seen that scares the birds is a hawk. One morning, I noticed the birds were quiet, too quiet. I came outside and found a giant red tail hawk perched on the rail above the fence where CeeCee is. It sat perfectly still and leered into the aviary. The strangest part was, the canaries held stock still. They did not move a muscle, they just seemed frozen. CeeCee showed up and helped me scare away the hawk but those canaries wouldn't move for hours after the hawk was gone. The hawk must have had very different intentions than CeeCee to scare them so."

"Very strange. Julia, I've been wanting to ask you something. Why do you want to be a nun?"

"Well, that's an interesting segue!" Julia laughed. "Lou, come here, let's sit down." Julia picked up CeeCee and they sat on a bench by the aviary. The canaries perked up and sang loudly for their new audience.

"To be honest, I've been asking myself why I want to be a sister ever since we ran into each other at the Convent, Lou. I've always wanted to join the convent, but now I have to admit I find myself thinking about you instead of my vocation." CeeCee jumped off Julia's lap and jumped back on the fence. Julia stood up slowly and brushed the furry white strands off of her

218

skirt. She went to the aviary and hooked her fingers through the mesh.

"I've wondered if God is testing me." She turned to him and said, "Seeing you here today… I'm more confused than ever."

Lou felt his heart beat a little faster and the hope he thought had dimmed was kindled. He cleared his throat, took another sip of soda.

"Julia, I can't tell you what to do, but I know you've prayed about this and I know, when a decision doesn't bring you peace, it's not the right decision."

"But I've *always* wanted to be a nun. I've always wanted to forget what I want and help people get what they need. It's who I am."

"It's not like they pay you," Lou said.

"I've never gauged my value on how much money people pay me, Lou. I just want to make a difference."

Lou looked around at the pots of winter flowers trimming the patio. His mother would have loved this garden. He stood up and went to Julia's side. The canaries quieted as he spoke softly next to her ear.

"Julia, I remember complaining to my mother about not being tall enough to play basketball. She told me something that stuck with me. She said God is like a gardener. Gardeners plant all kinds of flowers and plants. Some plants serve no purpose to the gardener; they are just pretty to look at. But, some plants are useful. My Mom used to plant chamomile and mint for tea; and basil, oregano and tomatoes for her pasta sauces. You know, some gardeners even plant attractive but poisonous plants. My mom wanted me to know that the gardener loves everything he plants, even if the

219

plants don't do anything for him, because each has a purpose. He plants them because he wants them in his garden. Or something like that, it's been a long time since she told me that story. The point is, I don't know a lot about God, but you should be what He made to be. If you were made to be a sister, you'll find peace in the Convent. If he made you to be my wife ..."

He put his soda down by CeeCee and took Julia's hands in his. He leaned forward until he could feel her breath on his mouth. If she moved forward just a little, the space between them would close and their lips would touch.

She stepped back, blushed and said, "Thank you, Lou. Your Mom was very wise. I guess I just need to decide what will bring me peace."

Lou was afraid he had swung too soon but kept his eye on the ball. He let go of her hands and held his arm out for her. She took it and they walked arm in arm to the front door.

"I'll be thinking about you," she said. She tipped up onto her toes to kiss his cheek. Lou smiled at her and went back to the truck.

Julia and the garden were behind him. He was sure of two things. He loved Julia so much that he wanted her to be happy, whether it was with him or without him. Second, it was time to take care of business. He had told Julia she would recognize the right decision if it brought her peace. He started the engine. He had a plan for peace.

Forty-one

CLEAN

IT WAS LATE in the day so El Camino was full of traffic. The red lights were long and the green lights were short. Lou rehearsed what to tell his Dad, holding nothing back in fear or shame.

He pulled into the back lot of the appliance shop and was not surprised to see, besides his Dad's delivery truck, an assortment of cars. There were two police cruisers, Exelda's Chevy Luv and a new Lexus. The vehicles were empty, so he assumed everyone was inside with his Dad.

He knew his Dad would not have invited a lawyer to the discussion, but Lou was ready to tell the whole truth even with the police there. An innocent person could incriminate himself talking to the police. Even a Miranda warning would not stop Lou from doing what he had to do.

The office was crowded with people, all of whom Lou knew. Dar was there, Exelda, and an old high school classmate who evidently had gone to the Police Academy.

"Hey Jim, you wearing the badge now? Who's watching you?" Lou joked.

"Hey Lou, long time no see, how are you?" the younger of the two police officers smiled and shook hands with Lou.

Frank interrupted the reunion, "Lou, we've got something serious going on here. You remember that diamond robbery at Dar's shop? Well, they think Exelda had something to do with it. They caught the male robber outside her flat in Los Alto. When the police asked why he was outside Exelda's place, he said it was because she has the diamond. He told the police Exelda was the woman who stole the diamond with him. He said he gave the diamond to her for safe keeping and now she has it."

"Mr. Dar thinks he recognizes Ms. Exelda and we're just curious about her involvement," said the older police officer, Officer Geraghty.

Dar objected, "No, no, no, I did not say she stole the diamond. I said, she looks like the woman who stole the diamond."

"Do you think she stole the diamond Mr. Dar?" asked Officer Geraghty.

"No, I do not think she stole the diamond, Officer, Sir. If Mr. Frank says she did not steel the diamond, then in that case, she did not steel the diamond," Dar said.

"But you were there, Dar, can't you tell the difference between Exelda and the thief?" Lou asked.

"Mr. Lou, I trust your father more than I trust my own eyes," Dar said. The police looked skeptically at each other, and Exelda held her eyes down. She wished she was invisible.

"Ms. White, I knew your Mom when she worked at the courthouse, she was a great woman and we all miss her. We don't suspect you in the diamond robbery; we just need to ask you a few questions. Do you know why the suspect who allegedly robbed Mr. Dar would be looking for you?" the younger officer, Jim McFadden asked.

Emboldened by the memory of her Mother, and by Frank's protective gaze she said in a polite but assertive voice, "No, Sir I don't. I don't live in the best of neighborhoods and I mind my own business."

Lou knew this scrutiny was unfair to Exelda and he determined to stop it. He cleared his throat and looked for water but there were no cups anywhere. His heart pounded as if he was on the edge of an abyss. He took a leap of faith.

"This might not be the right time to bring this up but, since we're all here ... I meant to call you guys, I mean call the police, but things got busy ... Anyway, I was in the Bicho Apartments this morning and I think you should know ..."

"Lou, does this have to do with the robbery?" Frank asked. He spoke in the tone of voice he reserved for commands and rhetorical questions. Lou was determined, however, and he continued, directing his comments to Officer Geraghty.

"I got into Apartment 309 using the key Jay, the apartment manager, gave me because there was no answer when I knocked on the door. Well, there was no answer because the tenant was dead."

Frank assumed Lou meant dead as in long ago gone so he stood up from behind his desk to interrupt before Lou blurted, "I could tell she was dead because, well, of course because she was staring at the ceiling ...

oh, and because of the gun. It must have been recent because the chair behind her head was still wet."

Lou surveyed the room and noticed a surprised but attentive look on each face. Frank sat back in his chair. Finally he had gotten through to them.

He would tell no one about the diamond in the dryer until he could talk to Exelda. She had been a family friend for as long as he could remember. If she had the diamond, he would give her a chance to explain herself.

"Do you mind coming down to the station so we can ask you a few questions, Lou?" Officer Geraghty asked, suddenly keenly focused on Lou.

"Is it really necessary to take him all the way to the police station?" Frank asked incredulous.

"Oh, yes, yes…" Officer Geraghty confirmed. Officer McFadden continued, "Yes, Frank, I think this time it really is necessary. Come on Lou, you can ride with me."

Lou hugged Exelda, told her not to worry, and left with the officers in the backseat of his old friend Jim's patrol car.

Forty-two

INTO THE LIGHT

EXELDA sat on the stool by the single window in her uncle's basement workshop. The window was covered by a bug screen and security gate. Looking out of the window, she watched a miniscule looking jet make a long, pink scratch on the dusky sky. A gnat caught between the window and the screen distracted her view. The fly flew in a straight line then in frenzied loops. She wondered how it had gotten trapped there.

It had been an exhausting day. It was comforting to hang out in her uncle's workshop in the basement of their flat. Frank had called her that morning and asked if she would talk to the police with him at his shop. He explained how the police had discovered the robber outside of her apartment, what he had told the police, and that Dar might have suggested she was involved in the robbery. She appreciated Frank's offer to clear things up for the police, but his protection felt impotent in the face of police suspicion.

"Well, well, well, would you look at this?!" Uncle Lamar exclaimed. Exelda glanced at her uncle who was finally scrapping the dryer from the Bichos laundry room. He held up what looked like a large chunk of glass.

"What you find this time Uncle, a rock?" she asked.

"Girl, I'm no jeweler but this looks like a diamond to me," he said. Exelda thought it was too big to be a diamond and besides, what would a diamond be doing in a dryer? Lamar brought it over to her. She held it up to the light from the window.

"Uncle Lamar, you know what that is? That's a diamond!" she exclaimed. Her Uncle laughed and Exelda soon joined in.

"Uncle, this diamond could pay for new windows in our church!" she said excitedly.

"Girl, that diamond would pay for new windows in a church *and* a house for us!"

"Wait a minute. Is that the dryer we got last week at Bicho Apartments?" she asked.

"Yeah, this is it. I couldn't take it apart 'til just now."

"Then that's the diamond that got robbed from Dar's shop!"

"Damn. You're probably right, Zelda. There goes the church windows. Do you think us finding this diamond after they already accused you of taking it will make us look bad, Exelda? They can't prove nothin' so maybe we shouldn't tell them. They'll think you stole it for sure."

"They already think I stole it because of what that thief said. Wait! Uncle Lamar, that's what he was doing prowling outside the flat! He was looking for this diamond! Uncle, I don't know what the police will do with me but Sundays ain't just for Sundays. We got to do the right thing and tell the truth no matter what happens to us. I mean happens to me."

"Exelda you're just like your mother. I could never change her mind and I know I can't change yours either. I just don't want you to get hurt, girl."He looked genuinely concerned. Exelda patted his hand. Suddenly, Exelda's cell phone rang.

"Exelda, it's Frank. The police just called. You're free and clear. Lou found a dead body over at the Bicho apartment and Dar identified the body. It was the female who helped rob his store. The prints on her gun match the male robber they caught by your place. They think he killed her because she couldn't produce the diamond. It was just a coincidence they caught him in your yard."

"Frank, it was no coincidence. Are you sitting down? Because you are not going to believe this. Lamar was taking apart the Bicho dryer just now and do you know what he found? Dar's diamond!"

"Wait a minute, what? Lamar pulled the diamond out of that old dryer? Are you serious?"

"I'm serious That poor dead woman must have put the diamond in the dryer before we took it away. That's why she couldn't produce the diamond for that bad man."

"Unbelievable. So, the killer knew you had the dryer and he was going to ... Oh, Exelda. He was capable of anything. I'm so sorry, I never should have involved you in any of this and... oh, I'm just so sorry."

"Frank, it's not your fault. But the next time you give me jewelry, I'll take it in a smaller box." Exelda said.

Frank laughed. "I wonder if Jay knew about the diamond and that's why he wanted the dryer back. Oh, but listen to this Exelda. Are you sitting down? Jay's

227

brother, Bob, found out how Jay was managing his apartment. The investigators working on the Coffee Shop case also uncovered Jay was skimming money from the maintenance fund. Bob fired Jay and asked us to get all the appliances in his building repaired or upgraded. Not only that, he wants us to get all the apartments in a new building he bought equipped and ready for occupancy. Are you ready for some new business?" Frank asked, "It's going to get busy."

Exelda did the math and was pleased to discover her money worries were over for awhile. "What about Lou? Is he OK?"

"Sure, he's fine, he's sitting right here in the office. I keep telling him he should be a police investigator, he's got a knack for mystery."

Lou smiled ruefully. How about repair? Did his Dad think he had a knack for repair?

Frank got off the phone and looked at Lou. The new business would allow Lou to build a nest egg for a family. Lou, father? Sometimes working with Lou was a little too exciting for Frank's temperament, but customers seemed to like Lou. The appliance business would probably continue to grow in his son's capable hands. He welled up with gratitude and pride. Yes, Lou would be a good father some day.

"I'm not sure I'm cut out for the appliance business, Dad. Trouble seems to follow me wherever I go," Lou said, shocking his Dad out of his reverie.

"What? Lou, listen to me. I don't tell you often enough, but I couldn't be prouder of you. I'm proud of what you're doing here. I told you, I got into some troubles myself. I need you here with me, son. You're

228

going to be the boss around here someday, I'm counting on you."

Lou's jaw hung in mid air and he did not bother to close it. He soaked in his father's words like a hungry sponge. Frank expected more animation from his usually positive son.

"Is there something bothering you, son?" Frank asked.

"Julia wants to join the Convent."

"Do you love her?"

"Sure I love her but I want her to be happy. I need to respect what she decides," Lou answered.

"Do you love her?"

"Dad, I told you I do."

"Then go get her." Frank reached in his pocket and pulled out the white box he had bought from Dar months ago. He took the ring out of the box. The remorse he felt for not giving it to Mae had tormented him since her death.

"Nobody ever failed trying. Take this and give it to Julia. I talked to Sister Martha today so I happen to know she's at the Convent."

"That's Mom's ring, Dad. You bought it for her. I can't take that."

"Yes you can. I just learned women like jewelry in small white boxes. Here." Frank put the ring back in the white box and held the box out until Lou took it. He smiled at his Dad, and left the shop.

Forty-three

CROSSED WIRES

WHEN SISTER MARTHA opened the door of the Convent, her expression was unreadable. She was not expecting Lou nor was she surprised to see him. She led him down the marble-floored hall to the doors of the Chapel.

"Julia is in here. I have some calls to make, will you be all right?"

"Sure I will Sister, no problem, thanks," he said and she continued down the hall alone. He opened one of the doors quietly and stood at the back of the vaulted room. In the middle of a sea of oak benches was Julia's kneeling figure. She was awash in blue and yellow light from the tall stained glass windows.

She had just come from a meeting with Mother Superior that released her from her intention to join the Convent. In reflection, Julia had felt peace at the thought of nurturing a family, but not at the thought of living in a Community of grown women. At first, she was very sad to let her life's ambition go. But this ambition was the only one she had allowed herself to pursue, not the only one she had. She prayed for a new direction.

"Julia," Lou said. His whisper carried in the quiet chapel. She turned to him and tears of joy began to flow so she put her head down to sob. Her prayers had been answered with Lou's arrival.

When Lou saw the tears, however, he kicked himself for being so stupid. She had come back to the Convent for good, he surmised. Her tears spilled from the guilt of hurting him. She planned her life before they met, why did he think she would change for him? He felt like an idiot, but saying so would make things worse for her.

"Julia, no, don't cry, you don't understand why I'm here." Lou hurried down the center aisle to her side. "I don't want you to worry about hurting me to be a nun. Even if you weren't joining the Convent, we both know we're not right for each other. We're too different from each other. Anyway, I was drinking that day I came over. I would have said anything. I get crazy when I'm drunk. I don't even have time for a girlfriend! So, just wanted you to know, I am glad you're turning into a nun."

Julia looked at Lou. Her hair was bedraggled and her eyes were red from nights of crying and no sleep.

"Really. Really? Well, that is considerate of you, Lou. How kind of you to make the trip to the Convent to tell me how you feel, which, of course is a relief because we are *very* different people. Well, I won't keep you. You see I have a lot of prayer I'm in the middle of here." She turned and did not look in his direction again.

Lou slinked out the back doors of the chapel and let himself out of the Convent. He drove back to the shop refusing to think of anything related to his future without Julia. If she was happy, he would be fine, and he would find happiness too.

"Lou, come in here, where are you going?"
Frank asked.

"To get the new door for the washer in Franklin Valley. I ordered a new one. By the way, it's no big deal but Julia and I are not "a thing" anymore, OK? It's a non issue, so let's move on; we don't need to talk about her anymore, OK?" Lou smiled at his Dad reassuringly and went to the supply room.

Forty-four

IN FRONT OF EVERYONE

THE CHRISTMAS day service at Exelda's church was a celebration of joy. The reward money for the diamond, which Lamar and Exelda donated to the building fund, had put the finishing touches on the building and the community reveled in it. The pastor danced with the choir and gave a joyful sermon on the baby Jesus in our hearts.

Of course, Frank and Lou attended their friends' celebration. Lou's attention to the preacher was thwarted by the presence of Julia in the church. She was invited to the festive service because her mother had donated to the building fund. Julia looked beautiful in a red dress which, Lou reminded himself, was appropriate for modern nuns.

When the service was over, the community gathered on the breezy church steps. Lamar attempted to extricate himself from a circle of senior, well dressed ladies wearing large, brightly colored hats. They surrounded Lamar and interrupted each other in an effort to capture his attention. Exelda posed for pictures with the Pastor, her niece, and her sister in front of a large flowerbed decorated in red flowers and holly bushes. The two widowers, Frank and Julia's fathers, had not seen each other since their respective wives' funerals. They both agreed it was better to meet under these happy circumstances. Julia and Lou stood next to their fathers but avoided eye contact with one another.

Suddenly, Dar burst from the church. Linda Straisburg, her new diamonds sparkling in the frosty sunlight, barely held onto his arm. He discovered Lou in the crowd, and rushed toward him.

"Lou! I have not seen you since you have become engaged! Your Father told me you would use the ring he bought at my shop!" Dar bear hugged Lou nearly lifting him off the ground despite being a head shorter than him.

Linda Straisburg worried that Frank felt jilted so she smiled apologetically at him. Julia squirmed uncomfortably at the unexpected news of Lou's engagement. She nudged her father in the direction of the car but Dar grabbed both of her hands before she could bolt.

"And this! This must be the beautiful Julia! Oh, Frank has told me so much about you! You are even more beautiful than I imagined, no wonder Lou loves you so much! Here, let me see the ring again, it's been so long!" Dar grinned widely and waited for Julia's enthusiastic response.

Julia stared wide eyed at the strange man who knew her name, and was so happy to see her. Lou was stunned. Seeing Julia in church was bittersweet and a little painful. Now Dar was twisting the emotional knife.

"Dar, please. This is *Sister* Julia McAuley. You know, like a nun? I'm really sorry, Julia," Lou said blushing.

"No, don't be sorry, I think there is a misunderstanding though. Lou, I decided not to become a sister." she said.

"Hey, I hear there's punch in the hall," Frank said. Dar looked at Linda, confused.

"I thought about what you said and it didn't give me peace when I thought of my future as a sister. So, I told Mother Superior, the day you and I met in the chapel, that I would not be joining the Convent." She had not seen Lou since that sad day and it felt good to finally reveal the truth to him.

Lou could not believe his ears. There she was, the woman who had won his heart in the laundry room of a Convent. The woman who knew how to start an antique ringer washer. The woman who was not a nun. The woman who made him feel …

Frank elbowed his son who seemed struck speechless for the first time in his life. Lou looked at his dad, then at Julia's dad.

"Sir, I love your daughter more than my own life. Her happiness is more important than my own. I want to marry her if she will have me." Mr. McAuley looked at his daughter. The joy in her eyes transformed her into the girl he remembered from happier days. He nodded in approval.

Lou put his hand in his pocket and felt for the ring box he had carried since the day he found Julia alone in the chapel. He knelt on one knee in front of her. He removed the sparkling ring from the box, and held it up to her.

"Julia McAuley, this was my mother's ring. You are the only woman I have ever loved besides her.

Please, take this ring, and me, so we don't waste anymore time being apart."

Julia held out her trembling finger and Lou placed the perfectly sized ring on it. He stood up and kissed her for the first time.

"Tell me those tears in your eyes are happy tears," Lou said

"Yes, they're happy tears," Julia said laughing.

"So, you'll marry me?"

"Oh, yes. I will."

CPSIA information can be obtained at www.ICGtesting.com
Printed in the USA
LVOW12s01062911l3

3631l3LV00014BA/237/P